"What Else Do You Remember?"
Cooper taunted.

To her credit, Kate flinched only a little. "Let's get it out in the open, Cooper. There's no point in dancing around something that never should have happened. I was a kid, but *you* weren't. You took advantage of me."

"Another Sinclair sin?" he jeered.

"Yes!" she shouted, then took a calming breath. "I didn't come here to debate the past with you. Just bear in mind that I'm not a kid now. You don't scare me anymore." She still felt intimidated by Cooper Sinclair, but she'd die before she'd let him know it.

"You got exactly what you wanted ten years ago."

"And you, Cooper Sinclair, are the same self-indulgent, conceited jerk I remember you to be. You're no different than your grandfather was. He took what he wanted, and so did you—only, he took Granddad's land and you took me."

MUSTANG VALLEY
Jackie Merritt

REUNION
WESTERN-
STYLE

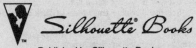

Published by Silhouette Books
America's Publisher of Contemporary Romance

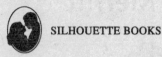

SILHOUETTE BOOKS

ISBN: 0-373-65317-4

MUSTANG VALLEY

First Silhouette Books printing September 1991

Visit Silhouette Books at www.eHarlequin.com

Printed in U.S.A.

JACKIE MERRITT

is still writing, just not with the speed and constancy of years past. She and her husband are living in southern Nevada again, falling back on old habits of loving the long, warm or slightly cool winters and trying almost desperately to head north for the months of July and August, when the fiery sun bakes people and cacti alike.

Please address questions and book requests to:
Silhouette Reader Service
U.S.: 3010 Walden Ave., P.O. Box 1325, Buffalo, NY 14269
Canadian: P.O. Box 609, Fort Erie, Ont. L2A 5X3

One

Sinclair's was packed with a typical weekend crowd, tourists in every conceivable costume from diamonds to cutoffs, locals in blue jeans and cowboy boots. Cooper Sinclair watched the main floor activity from a discrete vantage point, a small balcony that could only be reached from his private office. Sinclair's was unique in the world of modern-day Nevada casinos: the club was owned by only one man.

Cooper ran his place much like his grandfather, Sam Sinclair, had. The casino decor had changed little in forty years. The floors were still uncarpeted wood planks and the chandeliers were still the electrified wagon wheels that old Sam had originally installed. If people wanted crystal chandeliers and posh carpeting, they went to one of the enormous, glitzy hotel-casinos in downtown Reno. At Sinclair's, they got old-fashioned Nevada hospitality, smiles and excellent service, and the club had never had an unprofitable day since it opened in July of 1947.

The din from below, the jingling of coins, the whirring of slot machines, the bells when a jackpot was hit, shouts, laughter, the country music coming from the Maverick Saloon, a bar and lounge in the southeast corner of the club, all the cacophony of a busily engaged throng on a Saturday afternoon, had lost a little of its piercing stridency by the time it reached the second floor balcony. Still, Cooper winced a little over a group at a crap table screaming gleefully whenever the shooter made another successful toss of the dice.

He stood there a few more minutes, then turned and went into his office, closing the door securely. Instant silence ensued, the result of one of Cooper's few innovations to Sam's original design, soundproofing. The other changes during Cooper's reign had to do with accounting and record-keeping. While the business end of the successful operation had remained virtually untouched, computers now did in one-tenth of the time what bookkeepers had once labored incessantly over. Sinclair's second-floor administrative offices were as modern as any in town, a point of pride with Cooper, and the one aspect of the Sinclair family holdings where he and his grandfather had butted heads repeatedly.

With Sam's death three years before, once Cooper got over the initial grief of losing the most important person in his life, he had gone ahead with the improvements he'd always known were necessary. Today there were still accountants knee deep in work, but they handled the club's *and* the ranch's records with so much more efficiency, Cooper often wished old Sam were around to see it.

Thinking of his grandfather's weathered face and how much Sam had hated admitting he was wrong about anything, Cooper chuckled while he sat at his desk and reached for the phone. With the press of two buttons, he got Jack Leonard, his right-hand man. "Is the copter ready to go, Jack?"

"All set, Coop. I told them you'd be out to the heliport at two."

"Good. I'm ready to leave." He'd been ready for hours, dressed in the jeans, casual shirt, boots and corduroy jacket he preferred, but some details needing his personal attention had kept him at his desk until two.

"A limo's waiting at the south entrance. Have a good weekend, Coop."

"Thanks. I plan to. See you on Tuesday, Jack."

Using the staircase off limits to the public, Cooper descended to ground level. Outside, the wonder of a northern Nevada spring day struck him full force, and he breathed deeply of the fresh, warm air. A long weekend on the ranch was a glorious prospect, and one he didn't get to savor often enough anymore.

The limousine whooshed through the heavy weekend traffic, and after a few words with the chauffeur, Cooper settled back and let his thoughts wander where they may. For some reason—maybe because he'd just passed his thirty-fifth birthday—he'd been in a strange mood lately. Maybe he was reaching the age when a man begins to ponder his own mortality, he mused. Almost every one of his friends had been married at least once and most of them had children. Cooper Sinclair hadn't and didn't.

Not that he didn't have his pick of women. He was too mature and experienced to play games with himself when it came to his looks and appeal to the op-

posite sex. He knew very well that wavy black hair
and deep blue eyes were assets as far as attracting
women were concerned. He kept himself in good
physical shape, too. Not too many years ago there'd
been no reason to jog or work out; the ranch had taken
care of any excess weight. But after Sam's death, Cooper had had to spend more time in Reno, which had
meant fewer hours on a horse and less opportunity for
physical labor. He was still lean and lithe because of
a strenuous early morning run most days and three or
four hours a week working out in the gym he had
installed in his suite on the fifth floor of Sinclair's
Hotel and Casino.

Cooper had grown up in his grandfather's care and
didn't even remember his parents. They'd been killed
in a plane crash in Europe two years after his birth,
and whenever Sam had had one too many shots of
bourbon, he'd talked about losing his only son and
daughter-in-law with a tear in his eye. "They almost
took you with them on that trip," Sam would say
gruffly. "Thank the good Lord they didn't."

Sam had been an odd duck, Cooper had come to
realize, a strange mixture of attitudes. In business, Sam
had been hard-nosed and hardheaded, while at home,
within the privacy of the sprawling ranch house situ-
ated on six thousand acres of prime Nevada land, Sam
had been kindly and affectionate. Of course, he'd
loved a good argument, especially when Cooper had
mentioned computers. "I've lived sixty-seven years
without computers, boy," he'd say. "And I don't plan
to start complicating my life with machines at this
age."

Absently, staring out a window, Cooper reached
into the inside pocket of his gray corduroy jacket.

There was nothing there, and he grimaced at the long-time habit of reaching for a cigarette. He'd been trying to quit again, and empty pockets were one way of making a cigarette inaccessible when the urge struck. He felt antsy today, on edge and he was anxious to get out of town and in the air.

He piloted his own helicopter, a convenience to make travel between the casino and the ranch as easy as possible. But it had been three weeks since his last trip and he was more than ready for three days in the most beautiful, peaceful spot on God's green earth.

It took only a few moments to jump from the limousine and get settled in the helicopter, and less than five minutes more to go through his routine preflight check. Then he began snapping switches and pushing buttons, and the helicopter motor caught and the blades overhead began turning, slowly at first, then faster and faster. The copter lifted, and with the exhilaration flying always gave him, Cooper waved at the limo's driver, who'd stood by for the takeoff.

It was an hour before the helicopter even got near Sinclair land, but it was a trip that would have taken three times as long by car. Besides, getting a look at the country from the air was something Cooper never tired of. Range after range of mountains, the Trinity Range, Seven Troughs Range, the Humboldts, the distant and snowcapped peaks around Lake Tahoe, the deserts, Black Rock, Smoke Creek, the rivers and lakes, Cooper knew them all by name. This was his country and he loved it passionately.

His pulse quickened when he spotted Mustang Valley, still miles off but a lovely, misty patch of green between two ranges of mountains. He dropped down to three hundred feet and followed the Humboldt

River into the valley, gradually descending until the helicopter seemed to be skimming the tops of the old, gnarled cottonwoods along the riverbanks.

The red-tiled roof of the house appeared first, then Cooper could see the rest of it, creamy-white stucco exterior and courtyards, immense green lawn, cobalt-blue swimming pool. He breathed a sigh of satisfaction and anticipation. He was home.

After settling the copter on the ranch's helipad, Cooper jumped down to see Dirk Simons, the ranch foreman, coming out to meet him. "Hello, Dirk," he called.

"Hi, boss." Dirk grinned and offered his hand.

The two men shook hands. They spoke regularly on the telephone, so Cooper wasn't expecting any big news from Dirk. Still, as they walked toward the house, he asked, "How's everything?"

"Great, just great. Sheba had her foal last night, a colt."

Cooper chuckled softly. "Good for Sheba. I was hoping she'd throw a colt. Anything else happening?"

"Just a few phone calls and this." Dirk held out a business card.

Cooper took it and glanced at it. Then he stopped cold. "Where'd you get this?"

"She's waiting in the library, Cooper."

"She's here?" Cooper looked at the house, then read the card again. *Katherine A. Redmond, Attorney at Law.* He bypassed the letters after the name and checked the New York City address again with a frown. So, Kate Redmond had ended up in New York. Something stirred in him, memories, an image of long, honey-brown hair and green eyes, a mouth too sweetly curved to be believed, a slender, girlish body. "She wants to see me?" he asked softly, thoughtfully.

Dirk was younger than Cooper, twenty-eight to be exact, and he grinned now. "She's some looker, boss. She called last night and again this morning. Seems Leila knows her and told her you'd be here between three and four today. She arrived fifteen minutes ago."

Leila McCutcheon had been head housekeeper in the Sinclair household for at least fifteen years. Of course Leila knew Kate. She probably remembered Kate and her grandfather very well, although there hadn't been a Redmond living in Mustang Valley for more than ten years now.

Cooper started for the house again. "Thanks, Dirk," he called over his shoulder, suddenly anxious to see Kate Redmond again. The last time they'd seen each other had been a bitter battle, but she'd probably forgotten it the same as he had. There were other memories besides that final screaming match between them, some of them darned exciting to think about.

The helicopter's distinct sound had drawn Kate out of the library and into another room, a small den and office that had several windows from which to view the descending machine, then the man who climbed out of it. Cooper Sinclair. He was still good looking, damn him!

Through narrowed green eyes Kate watched Dirk Simons go out to meet his employer. The two men shook hands, talked briefly and started for the house. Backing away from the window just in case Cooper should happen to look at the den window and see her spying, Kate returned to the library and sat down.

Cooper Sinclair was not going to like the reason for

this visit, but it filled her, Kate Redmond, with a long hoped for, soul-satisfying elation. At last, at long last, she had it in her power to deal the Sinclairs a blow. Maybe nothing could entirely make up for what Sam Sinclair had done to the Redmond family, but this was going to help ease the old ache.

While Kate waited, she opened her purse, took a reassuring peek at the envelope within and snapped the purse's clasp closed again. Suddenly nervous and telling herself to calm down, she opened the purse again and withdrew a compact.

She'd spent two hours getting ready for this meeting, intent on looking her very best. Yes, her makeup was still perfect. Her nose didn't shine and her lips did, just the way she wanted them to. She patted the casually arranged curls around her face and dropped the compact back into her purse. Then she crossed one long, hosiery-sheathed leg over the other, smoothed the stark white, sharkskin fabric of her skirt, took a deep breath and composed her features.

Sounds from deeper within the house, muted voices, indistinguishable words, announced Cooper's arrival. Kate waited.

Cooper came to the open doorway and stopped. He took the sight of Kate Redmond in in one long, all-encompassing look, and felt as if someone or something had just struck him right between the eyes. The girl he remembered was no longer a girl; she was a beautiful, smartly dressed, extremely composed woman. Perhaps the green eyes were the only feature of her striking face that looked the same, startling in color, framed by their thick fringes of dark lashes, and yet they regarded him with a cool sophistication that certainly had only been acquired in the last ten years.

He knew he was staring and couldn't stop himself. "Hello, Kate," he said softly.

"Cooper," she acknowledged evenly.

He entered the room. "This is quite a surprise."

"I expected it would be."

Cooper still held the card Dirk had given him, and he glanced down at it for a moment. His gaze lifted. "So, you're an attorney."

"Yes."

"Should I presume this to be a business call, in that case?" Cooper spoke with amusement, because he couldn't even imagine a possible situation where Kate Redmond would have business to discuss with him.

He was startled to hear a cool "You should" from her. His amusement disappeared. "Perhaps you should enlighten me," he drawled, and sat in a chair directly across from her, patting his jacket pockets at the same time. There wasn't even one stray cigarette on his person. He glanced around, wondering if he'd left some here at the house. Any kind of pressure or stress brought about a restless craving for a smoke, and there was something about this little scene that was beginning to feel suspiciously stressful.

"I intend to do that," Kate replied in an emotionless voice.

Cooper held a hand up. "First, let me get you something to drink."

"No, thank you."

"Well, I need something. My throat's as dry as dust. Hold on a minute while I go get a beer." Cooper was out of his chair and gone in a flash, and Kate stared after him with a frown.

How dare he be even better looking than he'd been ten years ago! At twenty-five, the age he'd been when she'd left the valley, she had thought no man could possibly ever surpass Cooper Sinclair's dark good looks and flashing blue eyes. Even while she'd cursed him and every other Sinclair, both past and present, she had thought that. Nothing or no one had changed her mind, either, during the last ten years, and it was disgustingly irritating that Cooper's more mature thirty-five years had only enhanced an already outrageous handsomeness. She had actually prayed Cooper had lost his thick, unruly head of hair or developed a paunch.

He returned with a can of beer and a pack of cigarettes, and Kate smiled grimly. "Still trying to quit smoking?"

His smile was guilty, and yet he lit up. "Your memory's too good, Kate," he said through a cloud of smoke. Calmer, he took a swallow of cold beer. "I can't believe you're here."

"I'm going to be here all summer."

"You are?"

Kate stirred and uncrossed her legs. "I moved into the old house."

Cooper sat back, shock on his face. "That place is falling down. How could you possibly 'move in'?"

"No, it's not falling down. It needs paint and some repairs, but it's definitely not falling down." Deliberately, Kate let her eyes sweep the elaborate room. "It's not the Sinclair mansion," she added dryly, "but it will do for the summer."

Abruptly Cooper snuffed the cigarette out. It hadn't been the nicotine he'd needed, just the years' long habitual routine of lighting the damned thing. "What's this all about, Kate?" he asked with a little more force in his voice. "Your card has a New York address, and yet you're going to be here all summer? How come?"

The moment had finally come. A small smile hovered around Kate's glossy lips. "I've come to claim my water rights."

Premonition and an odd wariness hit Cooper. "What water rights?"

"Why, the water rights to Mustang Valley, of course."

A dark flush altered Cooper's color. "What in hell are you talking about?"

Kate recrossed her legs and settled back. "Perhaps I should fill you in."

"Yeah, maybe you should."

"I'm sure you remember my grandfather, Les Redmond? You'll remember him as the man *your* grandfather swindled out of fifty percent of this valley."

Cooper jumped up, immediately defensive. "No one swindled anyone out of anything, and you damned well know it!"

Dramatically Kate rolled her eyes upward. "I think we fought that battle ten years ago, Cooper, and if I remember correctly, neither of us backed down an inch. It would be pointless to go through it again."

"And immaterial and irrelevant, counselor?" Cooper snarled.

Kate's eyes snapped. "Oh, cut the theatrics, Cooper. The point is, you took Sam's side in everything he did, when, if you would have just opened your eyes a little, you would have seen what an old crook he was."

"It was *your* grandfather who was the crook," Cooper shouted, genuinely angry now. "Those two men made a deal, Kate, long before you and I were even glints in our folks' eyes. Hell, it was even before they were born! It was back in the twenties, when you couldn't even give land away. Your grandfather needed money and he came to Sam. Sam made him a loan, which probably saved old Les's butt. What made him think he never had to pay it back?''

Kate leaped up from the chair, eyes blazing. ''He tried to pay it back, damn you!''

''Sure, ten years too late,'' Cooper barked.

''He didn't have the money before that,'' Kate shrieked, then stopped, stunned by her outburst. She took a deep breath. ''This is exactly what I wanted to avoid. As you so sarcastically pointed out, it's immaterial what you or I think about it.''

Angry, as much with herself as with Cooper, Kate snatched up her purse and forced it open. With the envelope in her hand, she tossed the purse back onto the chair and swung around, facing the tall, blisteringly angry man again. Unabashed by glowering blue eyes and a terrible scowl, Kate said, ''Granddad died ten months ago. He left the little he had to me. I wish he would have allowed me to look through his papers a long time ago, because I found several very interesting documents.''

''Such as?''

Kate's chin came up even higher than it had been. ''The original declaration of homestead for one, explicitly listing the water rights for this valley. The other documents in this envelope are the mortgage Granddad gave Sam at the time of the loan and the final foreclosure papers. Nowhere in those two documents, *nowhere*, Cooper, is there one mention of water rights. Granddad never passed the water rights to Sam. He still owned them when he died, and now *I* own them. You, Mr. Sinclair, are using my water to raise your cattle and keep this valley green!''

Cooper stared blankly, then rushed forward. "Let me see those papers," he demanded angrily, and snatched the envelope from Kate's hand. She was trembling when she turned and walked to a window, but she knew Cooper was too involved in examining the envelope's contents to notice.

It was several minutes before she heard, "I don't believe this."

"Believe it," she suggested coldly as she turned around. "Those papers are legal and binding. You should know that. They're the same ones Sam used to kick the Redmonds off their own land."

Cooper's eyes were hard when he looked up from the papers. "He was more than fair with your family. Sam could have taken everything and he had the Redmond house and a hundred acres surveyed out of the foreclosure."

"A hundred acres when we owned three thousand," Kate snapped. "How would you like to be billed for all the water you've used for the past ten years? That's what Sam would have done to anyone who'd destroyed him the way he did Granddad."

"Is that what you're going to do, send me a bill?" Cooper snarled.

"Even you might have trouble paying a bill of that size," Kate exclaimed heatedly.

"Then again, maybe I wouldn't," Cooper muttered, and shoved the papers back into the envelope. "I want my attorney to look at these. Any objections?"

"They're only copies. Show them to anyone you please."

Cooper watched her pick up her purse from the chair. "What do you want, Kate?"

"Want?"

"Yes. If the papers are legal and binding, as you claim, what do you want for them?"

Her eyes blazed again. "I want Redmond land back, free and clear."

"That's blackmail!"

"That's business!" Kate started for the door, but stopped before she reached it. "You have this summer to check the legality of the papers and make a decision. I plan to stick right here, Cooper. I took a leave of absence from the law firm I work for. This was much too important to me to handle from New York."

"I'm sure it was."

They stared at each other with cold animosity. "Sam was too shrewd to overlook something as crucial as water rights," Cooper spat.

"Obviously he wasn't as shrewd as you give him credit for. This is the kind of mistake that lawsuits are made of. The courts are full of just such mistakes," Kate said dryly.

"And you should know, right? How in hell did you get to be an attorney?"

Kate's eyes flashed again. "It wasn't because I inherited a pile of cash and property like you did. I worked my tail off to get through college and law school."

He flushed at her derision. "Whether you want to admit it or not, I worked my tail off, too. Being Sam Sinclair's grandson didn't mean a free ride, which you know as well as I do. Don't stand there and pretend you don't remember that I worked as hard on this place as any other cowhand."

Some of Kate's anger abated. "You're right. I'm sorry I made that crack. I remember how hard you worked very well."

Something hot and cruel had invaded Cooper's system. He wanted to shake the composure she clung to despite the aggravated emotions they'd ruffled in each other. "What else do you remember?" he taunted, and gained the small satisfaction of seeing Kate Redmond lose a shade of coloring. She knew what he was talking about, *exactly* what he was referring to.

To her credit, she flinched only a little. "Let's get it out in the open, Cooper. There's no point in dancing around something that never should have happened. I was a kid, but *you* weren't. You took advantage of me."

"Another Sinclair sin?" he jeered.

"Yes!" she shouted, then took a calming breath. "I didn't come here to debate the past with you. Just bear in mind that I'm not a kid now. You don't intimidate me anymore." *Oh, yeah?* a small voice mocked in her head. She still felt intimidated by Cooper Sinclair, by the same traits he'd overwhelmed her with years ago and still possessed in abundance, good looks and a cocky confidence. But she'd die before she'd let him know it.

With a black look on his face, Cooper slowly advanced. "I don't, huh? Well, maybe I should." He held the envelope up right in front of her face. "I'm not taking this sitting down, Kate. First, I don't believe it. There's a piece missing, something that even a smart New York lawyer like you think you are has overlooked. Second, if you'd have come here without that chip on your shoulder, we might have worked this thing out without a battle. And third, I didn't take advantage of you. You got exactly what you wanted ten years ago, and it galls the bloody hell out of me that you've twisted the past around to suit your own purpose.''

"And you, Cooper Sinclair, are the same self-indulgent, conceited bastard I remember you to be,'' she sputtered angrily. "You're no different than Sam was. He took what he wanted and so did you, only he took Granddad's land and you took me.''

"I took what was offered, honey. Offer it again and see what happens,'' he taunted in a sneering challenge.

Kate was breathing hard with the most consuming fury of her life. She had planned this meeting for months now, visualizing the pleasure of besting a Sinclair. But she should have known Cooper would pervert the situation with reminders of the passion that had once torn her apart. "I loathe and despise you,'' she hissed, and spun around to leave.

Cooper watched her go through the doorway, then he sprang forward and followed, tracking her swaying hips from three steps behind. Anger knotted his guts, but even in the swirling red mist behind his eyes he saw her straight back, her small waist, her flaring female behind and her trim legs below the hem of her white skirt. It didn't seem possible that this expensively dressed, ripely beautiful woman was the Kate he remembered. How old was she now, about twenty-eight, twenty-nine? Certainly no more than thirty. How old had she been under the stars that night, eighteen? Or, had she been younger?

No matter, she riled him like no one else ever had.

Kate had known he was following her, but she hadn't thought that Cooper would dare to touch her. Gasping in shock, she found herself up against a wall, with Cooper effectively trapping her, his hands on the wall on each side of her head, his eyes dark blue and glaring. She could feel the heat of his anger, the heat of his body, and a strange fear shot through her system.

"So, you hate and despise me," he ground out. "That's what you said that night by the river, too, but it didn't stop you from writhing under me, did it?"

"You beast," she whispered, shaken to her very soul.

"Maybe that's the real reason you're back here stirring up trouble," he mocked raggedly. "Maybe you'd like to stir up something else. Would you, Kate?" She'd turned her face away, and he took her chin and forced her to look at him again. His eyes were hot and harsh looking, without a trace of gentleness. "I dare you," he rasped. "I dare you to do what you really want."

She found a voice, a tense, derisive one. "I fully intend to do what I really want, and it has nothing to do with what's in your dirty mind."

"Dirty mind? That's funny, baby, really a hoot. You didn't think I had a dirty mind down by the river that night. You couldn't get enough of me. We made love for hours, as I recall."

Her face was on fire. "I don't need you to remind me of the most debasing experience of my life!"

"Oh, so now it's debasing. What was it that night, Kate? I don't think you were labeling it debasing then."

"Get away from me! I'd like to leave."

He stared at her. There was still anger in the air, hot and heavy, but there was something else, too. He felt it coursing through his veins and tensing his loins.

Kate felt it, too. He could see it in her eyes, smell it
in her scent. It was the same thing that had built and
built and finally consumed them before, desire, passion, pure unadulterated lust for each other.

"Well I'll be damned," he said softly. "It's still
between us, isn't it?"

"No!" she cried, refusing to be drawn into the scenario. She'd been so sure, so positive that she'd feel
nothing except triumph at this meeting. Cooper had
provoked almost every emotion she possessed, and
now he was trying to draw her into another tasteless
sexual encounter. "For God's sake, let me leave," she
moaned.

"Yes," he said suddenly, harshly, and dropped his
hands and stood back. "Go on, get out of here before
I do something we'd both regret."

Kate rushed to the door and jerked it open. Tears
scalded her eyes and blurred the sidewalk to the driveway. Her hands were shaking and the trembling continued throughout her body. She was still no match for
Cooper Sinclair, she realized, and wondered why she
had thought she could handle him any better now than
she had ten years ago.

Two

The drive back to the old Redmond homestead took only a few minutes. Kate muttered to herself as she followed the dusty driveway, "It's *not* falling down," resentful that Cooper would even make such a disparaging remark. Of course, by Sinclair standards, the two-storied, twin-gabled brown shake house was probably an eyesore. Even dilapidated, though, it was important to her, filled with poignant memories. The old place represented the sum total of the first eighteen years of her life, after all.

She had been there four days already, time she had spent in cleaning, getting started on some much needed painting and gathering her courage for today's confrontation. It was funny that while still in New York, contemplating tossing her bombshell in Cooper's face had been wildly energizing, but once in Nevada, back in Mustang Valley, she had actually needed to bolster her courage.

Small wonder, Kate admitted grimly as she pulled the car to a stop beside the house, furious again over the past half hour. Maybe her conscious mind had forgotten Cooper Sinclair's rude command of most situations, but her inner self had obviously had more sense. To think they had once been friends!

Well, that wasn't entirely accurate, either. The relationship she had endured with Cooper Sinclair had been a hot and cold alliance at best, and to be brutally honest, it had been mostly cold. To him she'd been the pesky girl on the next ranch, someone to tease and sometimes take a horseback ride with when he didn't have something better to do.

Kate had known full well when Cooper had been between girlfriends. Girls had always flocked his way, and when he'd been involved with one he'd stayed away from the Redmond place. Kate had told herself again and again during those sometimes extended absences that the next time Cooper showed his face she was going to shout him into oblivion with a blast of cuss words. She knew the words, too, and they had begun with ''You can go straight to hell, Cooper Sinclair!'' and ended with some that might have made a sailor blush.

A few times she'd even done it, but Cooper had only laughed and teased her out of her mood, inviting her to take a ride with him in the next breath. She'd always relented and gone, unable to deny herself the furtively exciting pleasure of again exploring the valley they both knew as well as the back of their own hands with Cooper riding beside her.

Those memories lived in Kate's mind beneath those

she had acquired later. At twenty-eight she knew she had been a tomboy in those days, but at the time she hadn't given her immutable uniform of jeans and boots a thought. She had grown up on a ranch and been a product of its earthy life-style, just as surely as the spring calves and the annual crop of wild hay. She realized later, after she'd seen something else of the world, that Cooper must have viewed her in a way she hadn't even been capable of visualizing at fifteen or sixteen. To the teenaged Kate Redmond, riding a horse like a wild thing, her long hair billowing out behind her, had been merely who and what she was. Later, in retrospect, Kate saw that she'd been a free-spirited, barely tame creature, comfortable only with her grandfather and, occasionally, Cooper Sinclair.

The big empty house echoed her footsteps as Kate went in and slammed the front door with unnecessary force. So far her efforts to make the place livable for the summer had been confined to the first floor, and the fumes of fresh paint and lemon-scented soap greeted her, a vast improvement over the musty, dusty atmosphere she'd encountered on her initial arrival.

Storming into the room she'd fixed up for a bedroom, what had originally been her grandfather's office, Kate tossed her purse on the bed and began to undress. Why she had thought it necessary to face Cooper looking like a fashion model was beyond all ability to reason in her present state of mind. The white suit had cost a small fortune, likewise the accessories, Italian-made black and white leather pumps and purse. The desire to look her best no doubt had roots in the old memories hounding her, a burning desire to let him know she was no longer the jeans' clad, wild-eyed teenager she'd been ten years ago.

Well, he'd taken it all wrong, as she should have known he would. *Maybe you'd like to stir up something else,* he'd taunted, practically saying right out that she'd come back because of him. He was no different now than he'd always been, conceited, egotistical, overbearing.

When she had first gone through Les's papers, the water rights implication had completely escaped Kate. It had been several weeks later, while reading a client's file who was in the midst of a legal battle over water rights on a piece of Arizona property, that it had occurred to her that something was amiss in her grandfather's old documents.

It had taken a half dozen long-distance calls to Carson City and to the county courthouse to finally accept what had initially seemed utterly impossible: Sam Sinclair had definitely gained possession of the Redmond land, but while he had also assumed all rights to the water in the area, he had never legally acquired them. More precisely, Les Redmond had never relinquished his ownership by legal conveyance. Half of the valley's water rights belonged to Les Redmond's heirs, and there was only one, Kate.

Cooper's swift challenge about a missing piece in the transaction had occurred to Kate, too. But if there was something missing, she hadn't been able to find it. And she'd been very thorough. It had taken weeks to assimilate all the information she had gathered, mostly because Kate knew her grandfather had been no more aware of what she'd discovered than she had been. What she'd stumbled upon was a mistake, she had finally realized, a fluke, and as she'd told Cooper, the kind of chance occurrence that lawsuits were made of.

It was at that point Kate began thinking of facing Cooper with the power she'd suddenly been given. Without ample water, his Mustang Valley ranch would be worth much less than it was. Without enough water, some of the green fields would dry up and revert to sagebrush and bunchgrass, and the size of his cattle herds might even have to be decreased. The prospect carried a certain amount of satisfaction, but was that all she wanted?

She'd had to think long and hard on the matter. Devaluing the ranch would not destroy the Sinclair empire. It was Sinclair's in Reno that had made Sam Sinclair wealthy, not the ranch. The ranch had been his pride and joy, true, just as it probably meant a great deal to Cooper today, but it wasn't what had made the Sinclairs millionaires many times over.

Striking a financial blow wasn't her best weapon, Kate had decided. And remembering her decision while she undressed, Kate admitted it again. In anger she'd hurled a threat about sending Cooper a bill for the water he'd used in the past ten years and it had caused only a mild reaction. Demanding Redmond land back, though, had vigorously raised Cooper's hackles!

A slender thread of glee mingled with the clouded emotions choking Kate. She'd struck a nerve with that demand, all right. Cooper would show the papers to his legal advisers, but Kate was confident no one could find anything more in them than she had. Once Cooper admitted he was cornered, he'd have to talk to her again.

Kate's blood raced at the thought. Today he'd managed to turn the focus of their meeting with a disgusting reference to that long-ago night by the river.

She should have anticipated such crudity and been better prepared. Instead of humiliated anger, she should have remained cool and unaffected. Next time, she would. And there definitely would be a next time, only *she* would have the upper hand. She already had it, but it would take conferences and time with his attorneys for Cooper to know it.

Kate hung the white suit in the closet and pulled on some work clothes, a pair of paint-spattered yellow shorts and an old sleeveless white blouse that she tied at her midriff. Brushing her hair away from her face, she secured it with a rubber band at the back of her neck, then slipped her feet into canvas sneakers. She went to the kitchen, ready to get back to the unfinished chore of giving the old cabinets a coat of fresh paint.

Cooper prowled the house, moving from room to room with the restless energy of a hungry jungle cat. The quiet weekend he'd wanted so badly was impossible now; Kate had very neatly shattered the peace of Mustang Valley and his own nerves.

He didn't believe either her or those damned documents. As he'd told Katherine A. Redmond, Attorney at Law, there had to be a missing piece. Old Les's water rights could have been conveyed in a separate document. Cooper was positive that whatever had happened more than ten years ago, there had to be an explanation for the situation. Sam never would have overlooked such a critical point.

Cooper debated whether to hop in the helicopter and head right back to Reno and his attorneys or wait until Tuesday. Some obstinate inner voice told him there was no need to rush away. He'd come for the weekend and he needed a break from the business and the traffic and the hordes of people. In completely honest moments, Cooper knew he was getting more fed up with the casino atmosphere every day. He certainly didn't need the money that increased his bank account every month, and it was getting harder and harder to force himself to stay in Reno when he wanted to be in Mustang Valley.

For the past year Cooper had been giving serious thought to selling Sinclair's. It was sentimental loyalty to Sam's memory that kept getting in the way of the decision, he knew. Sam had loved the place. He would walk through the casino and slap strangers on the back as if they were old friends. Many times Cooper had seen his grandfather fish a ten or twenty out of his own pocket and lay it on top of someone's bet at a twenty-one table. "For luck," Sam would declare, and if the gambler won the hand, Sam would walk off laughing, leaving the increased winnings for his newly made friend. It was things like that that had made Sinclair's so successful, and Cooper knew that Sam was greatly missed in Reno.

But he wasn't Sam, and he had never shared his grandfather's affection for noise and confusion. Cooper's heart was in Mustang Valley, and he didn't get back to the ranch nearly enough.

He finally decided to stay for the weekend as he'd planned. Feeling somewhat more settled on the matter, Cooper went to his suite, took a shower and stretched out on the bed, one arm crooked beneath his head while he stared at the ceiling.

Kate Redmond. Katie, as he'd often called her, had turned out to be an incredibly attractive woman. Maybe the promise had always been there. As a teenager her hair had been long and straight and the most bewitching shade of sun-kissed light brown he'd ever seen. She had been able to outride most men, getting the most out of a horse with an almost careless control. They'd had some great times together, but maybe Kate had forgotten them because of what happened that one night.

Stirring, Cooper's features compressed into a frown. Maybe he *had* taken advantage of Kate that night. He'd been older by seven or eight years and certainly had known the ropes. Kate hadn't. She'd been a virgin, a fact that hadn't sunk in until it was too late. He remembered the whole incident very well, now that he put his mind to it.

Sam had filed the foreclosure papers, and earlier that day Kate had screamed her fury at Cooper when he'd stopped by. Sometimes her mouth had shocked him. She'd been a wild little thing, used to men and men's talk, and some of the things that came out of her pretty lips could have blistered paint. That day she'd been in rare form and had denigrated the Sinclairs in a dozen nasty ways. Cooper had shaken his head in disgust and ridden off, leaving her standing in the Redmond yard still screaming and flailing her arms at him.

By the evening he'd hoped she had cooled off. Despite understanding Sam's loss of patience with Les Redmond, Cooper had felt bad about the matter. He'd saddled his horse and ridden back to the Redmond place.

Only, when he approached a crook in the river, there was Kate. She was sitting on the bank and dangling her bare feet into the water. Cooper had reined his horse and sat silently for a moment. There was no way she could have missed hearing him come up, but she'd kept her face turned away.

"Kate?" he said softly.

"Go away."

He heard the agony in her voice, and after a hesitation he got off his horse and went over to her, hunkering down on the riverbank beside her. *"Don't hate me,"* he pleaded.

"I hate you with every breath in my body," she returned dully.

"Why? Kate, I've done nothing to you." He put a hand on her shoulder, and she shook it off as if it were something poisonous.

"Keep your hands to yourself! Go put them on one of your girlfriends!"

He studied her slender form and the curve of her cheek, all he could see of her in the waning light. *"We're friends, Kate. What our grandfathers do to each other shouldn't change that."*

She whirled, giving him a view of reddened, swollen eyes. *"You're exactly like Sam. Don't you dare pretend you're not a part of this."*

He ignored her accusation. *"You've been crying."*

"No, really?" she drawled sarcastically. *"I wonder why. Do you think you wouldn't cry if you were suddenly thrown out of the valley?"*

"You haven't been thrown out of the valley."

"Oh, leave me alone! Get back on your damned horse and go away!"

He should have listened to her, Cooper thought with a strange emptiness. He should have immediately gotten back on his horse and left Kate alone.

Instead he'd made love to her. He'd pulled her into his arms to soothe her and ended up making love to her.

A long-forgotten guilt curled within him, compounded by a new one, the way he'd taunted Kate over that night just today. What he should have done was apologize. Was it any wonder she hated the Sinclairs? Even if Sam had been well within his rights to fore- close on Redmond land, his grandson hadn't had the right to violate Kate Redmond. And he could tell him- self a thousand times that Kate had wanted just what he had, but he'd been old enough to maintain a clear head and he hadn't done so.

Uneasily Cooper swung his feet to the floor. Maybe it was time for that long-neglected apology. Kate had taken him by surprise today and he'd reacted with an- ger, justified perhaps by what she had dropped on him without warning. But even if her documents had merit, the problem would be resolved a whole lot easier with- out that other animosity between them.

Besides, if she was back in the valley for the sum- mer, she should be given some kind of welcome sign. After all, old Les and Sam had homesteaded Mustang Valley together, and just because their relationship had deteriorated to the point of uncompromising dislike for each other, that didn't mean he and Kate had to keep the old feud going. They were adults and had been friends once; surely she didn't want hostility in the valley any more than he did.

Yanking out clean jeans and a white shirt from the closet, Cooper dressed quickly. Choosing his favorite old riding boots, he grabbed up a gray Stetson and plopped it on his head. He'd go to Kate and see if some of those old, battered fences could be mended.

The late afternoon sun had raised the thermometer level to a breathless ninety-two degrees. Usually the valley was cooled by a pleasant westerly breeze, but today the air was still. Taking a break, Kate sat on the back porch with a glass of iced tea. There was white paint in her hair, on her face and on her hands, but she hadn't scrubbed it off because she planned to work a few more hours before she quit for the day.

Maybe the place is falling down, she thought sadly as her gaze swept the dust and patches of crisp, yellowed grass that had once been lawn around the house. Shrubbery bordering the yard had died, too, and only some obstinate cottonwood trees still had life in their gnarled branches. Sitting so quietly, Kate spotted several tiny rodents, desert gophers, running through the parched, weedy grass, and a little further out, a jackrabbit. Sinclair cattle and horses grazed well within sight, kept away from the buildings by a double strand of barbed wire. Kate knew that her grandfather hadn't put up the fence, so the Sinclairs must have fenced the place, a small enough consideration after everything else they'd done.

Bits and pieces of the telephone calls Kate had made to Nevada from New York flitted through her mind. One clerk in the assessor's office of the county courthouse had been particularly chatty, and Kate had learned of Sam Sinclair's death and Cooper's bachelorhood without even asking. At the time she'd been genuinely surprised, having supposed beforehand that Cooper surely must have married since her departure.

She hadn't, of course, but then she was years younger and had plenty of time for marriage. Then, too, she had never had quite the affinity for the opposite sex that Cooper had. Relationships weren't easy for Kate. She took them much too seriously, and in doing so had several times scared herself by becoming too involved with a man she hadn't really loved. Gradually she had come to understand herself a little better and began to maintain purely platonic associations with the men she occasionally dated. At present, there was no one even remotely special in her life.

But Cooper's single status was a puzzle. Kate would have bet anything that he'd gotten married a long time ago.

Sighing, she took a swallow of cold tea, allowing one of the ice cubes to pass between her lips to melt in her mouth. Without a breeze rustling leaves and dried shrubbery, it seemed quieter than usual. Even Cooper's cattle and horses were barely moving in the still, hot atmosphere, and many of them were lying down in the lush grass of their pasture.

Then, off in the distance, Kate heard a dog's playful yaps. She scanned the fields and her eyes narrowed on a tiny silhouette of a horse and rider. It was a man, she was certain, and it took only a few moments of staring before she recognized which man. Cooper. And he was coming her way.

No, that wasn't necessarily true. He could be merely checking his outer range, what had once been Redmond range. Surely he wouldn't have the audacity to drop in after that fiasco at his house, would he?

Squinting suspiciously, Kate watched. The horse was walking, so Cooper apparently was in no hurry, wherever he was going. The dog she had heard became more than a speck of bouncing excitement as it darted back and forth around the horse's hooves, and after another few minutes Kate saw that it was another of the red hounds the Sinclairs had always favored.

"Damn it, he *is* coming here," Kate muttered, instantly blasted with dread and a curling warmth in her belly. Involuntarily her hand went to her hair and she caught sight of the blotches of white paint on her fingers. There were spatters on her thighs, too, and she'd already seen the mess she'd accidentally smeared in her hair. She looked as opposite to the well-dressed, perfectly put-together woman she'd been earlier as she possibly could, and for a moment she thought of running into the house and locking the doors and to hell with what Cooper Sinclair might think of her evasiveness.

But she couldn't do that. She had to stand her ground with Cooper wherever or whenever they happened to meet. He might construe evasiveness as fear, and she'd go back to New York tomorrow rather than let him think she was afraid of him.

Nothing said she had to be hospitable, though. She owed him nothing, and if he wanted to stand around on her back porch like a lost sheep while she coolly dealt with whatever he'd come for, that was up to him.

She sipped from the glass of iced tea and sat perfectly still.

Cooper didn't notice her at first. The ride over had been pleasant despite the glare of the hot sun, and he'd also enjoyed the hound's joyful leaps and bounds. Any time he rode around the ranch, one or more of the dogs followed along, so both he and his horse, Monty, were used to a dog cavorting underfoot.

Cooper spied a white sedan and remembered seeing it, from the helicopter, in his own driveway earlier today, although it had aroused no particular suspicion at the time. It should have, he thought wryly, remembering again Kate's startling information. As certain as she was about the water rights, though, he was equally as certain she was wrong.

He checked the old house out as he got nearer and

shook his head, questioning Kate's good sense. Les Redmond had never been much of a handyman, and even during his residency the place had always needed repairs. Ten years of vacancy had only compounded already noticeable decay.

Les had been a strange duck, too, Cooper mused, just as odd in his way as Sam had been in his. They'd had similarities, gruffness concealing tender feelings toward their own, a penchant for good bourbon and cigars, and rough exteriors. Beyond those traits they'd been very different men. Sam had been economically ambitious, farsighted enough to take advantage of Nevada's unique gambling laws. It was Sinclair's that had made Sam a wealthy man. Les, on the other hand, had been content to desultorily run a cattle ranch, and no one ever attained success on a cattle ranch without a lot of hard work and dedication.

While Sam and Les had started out equal, Sam had pulled way ahead in the financial department. Perhaps that was what had ultimately caused the breach between the two men, Cooper pondered, remembering the final bitterness his grandfather and old Les had had for each other.

Well, it would be juvenile and petty for he and Kate to embellish upon or even recognize those old hurts. True, they had headed in that direction today. But now that he'd had time to think, he sure didn't want to dwell on the past. Hopefully, Kate felt the same way deep down.

The red hound suddenly took off, and Cooper saw him bounding for the house, slowing down only a little to slither under the lowest strand of barbed wire. Then he was running again, and yapping as though on the scent of something. That's when Cooper saw Kate on the porch. She let the hound sniff her, then seemed to be welcoming him with a pat on his head.

Rather solemnly, wondering just how Kate was going to take this visit, Cooper rode to the stock gate, unhooked it and passed through. He relatched it and rode closer to the house. Kate gave her attention to the hound, but unobtrusively she missed none of Cooper's movements. She saw him dismount and approach on foot.

Cooper stopped at the porch stairs. "Mind if we talk a little?" He was staring, seeing a much different woman than had invaded his home earlier today. This Kate was much closer to the one he remembered, looking very much like the girl she'd been ten years ago. Something stirred within him, a physical reaction to a memory. That night by the river Kate had been soft and warm…but only after the wildness of passion had subsided. This afternoon she'd been coolly distant; now she presented a combination of all the diverse qualities she possessed.

Her eyes flicked upward briefly, showing him nothing of what she might be thinking. "What about?"

Cooper looked off, then back to her. He maintained casualness though he was seeing, probably for the first time, the complexities of Kate's personality. "The past, the future, whatever. I just think we should communicate, Kate."

Who was he trying to kid? He was worried! Elation brought a spark to Kate's eyes. Stroking the hound's ears, she nodded. "I guess we can talk," she allowed quietly, concealing her triumph.

Cooper climbed the few stairs and leaned his hips against the porch railing. There was only the one chair on the porch, and Kate knew she should bring another one out from the kitchen. But she restrained the impulse and continued petting the dog. "What's this one's name?" she asked.

"Rusty. What have you been doing, painting?"

"That's rather apparent, isn't it?"

"What are you painting?"

"The kitchen cabinets."

"You really are planning to spend the summer here?"

Kate lifted her gaze from the hound. "Does that prospect bother you?"

"Why should it bother me? This is your property."

"Yes, it is. When did you put up the fence?"

"Right after you and Les left. It didn't seem right to have cattle running all over your land."

Kate couldn't prevent a dryly stated, "That was big of you."

A grin tugged at the corners of Cooper's mouth. "It kills you to admit the Sinclairs might have done something considerate, doesn't it?"

"What it does is surprise me," Kate shot back.

"Nobody could be as bad as you think the Sinclairs have always been, Kate."

"Oh, really? Now why do I have a little trouble believing that?"

"I wouldn't know."

Smirking, Kate glanced up at Cooper. "Obviously you came over here to play some kind of silly game."

"No, I came to mend fences. And I'm not talking about that string of barbed wire out there, either."

Kate sat back, ignoring the dog. Rusty looked at her questioningly for a moment, then dashed off the porch in chase of a gopher. Watching the hound's antics, Kate said tonelessly, "I have enough money to pay

Granddad's debt. I don't expect to get my land back for nothing."

Cooper raised an eyebrow. "Do you want to go to court over this thing?"

"No, but I will if that's what it takes. And I would win, Cooper. Those water rights were never conveyed. Legally, I own them."

"And morally?"

Kate's face pinkened slightly, but her eyes flashed just as the flush darkened her cheeks. "I'm surprised you have the nerve to bring up morality."

Cooper looked off across the yard for a moment. "You're right on that point. I never should have touched you." His gaze came back to Kate. "I'm sorry for that, Kate. An apology can't change what happened, but I want you to know how sorry I am for it. I apologize for what I said today, too. It wasn't fair to put some of the blame for that night on you. I was old enough to know better and you were just a kid."

The pink in Kate's cheeks had faded. She didn't want nor did she believe the apology. But that wasn't what was wrenching her emotions. She'd been a kid in years, that was very true, but what she'd felt for Cooper had been as far from childlike as anything could be. In a way she hadn't understood back then, she had idolized him. She understood it now—for what it was worth, which wasn't much, not the way things stood today. They were worlds apart, and she was back for only one reason: to reclaim her grandfather's land. Cooper could deem it immoral or unethical or anything else he damn well pleased; she fully intended on seeing justice done.

Kate purposely kept a closed expression on her face.

"I'd rather not talk about apologies, if you don't mind. Whatever happened is long in the past."

Cooper studied her. "You're being ambivalent. How can you claim a desire to forget the past when you're here because of it?"

His astuteness unnerved her and she reacted with anger. "Yes, I am. But I'm not going to allow you to keep clouding the real issue with unnecessary detours. If you really mean that apology, prove it by forgetting that disgusting incident out by the river ever happened."

"Disgusting?" Frowning, Cooper pushed away from the railing and turned his back to Kate. He dug his hands into his jeans' pockets and stared off into the distance. "You know," he said softly, "it's pretty obvious you and I remember that night differently. It was neither debasing, which you called it earlier today, nor disgusting, to me. I'm sorry you remember it that way."

Startled, Kate said nothing, and when Cooper turned around again, she met his eyes without a whole lot of courage. For several seconds their gazes held, and the atmosphere suddenly seemed weighted with the hours they had spent in each other's arms beside the river on that beautiful summer night so many years ago.

An initial embrace, which Kate had tried to elude, had exploded into fiery passion. If she'd been more experienced she might have been able to stop what had ensued. Or would she have stopped it even then? She had participated eagerly, hungrily, and both of them knew that, even if Cooper was now willing to shoulder all the blame.

Kate wet her lips. "Just forget it," she whispered hoarsely. "Please just forget it."

Cooper's eyes were darker. "I thought I had. Until today I think it was forgotten. You brought it all back. I'm having some strange thoughts about the matter now. It was pretty meaningful, Kate."

She attempted sarcasm. "How could it have been meaningful for a man with a dozen women on the string?"

"Good question," Cooper replied quietly.

Her chin came up. "I know why you're doing this and it won't work. I'm not going to be swayed from the real reason I'm here by good looks and charm and clever innuendo."

"Oh? You think I'm good looking? And charming?" he drawled with amusement.

"You know damned well you are!"

"I see. Well, so are you. You're not just good looking, Kate, you're a beautiful woman."

She turned her face away. "Oh, for crying out loud," she muttered, and heard him say, "You're afraid of me, aren't you?"

"I most certainly am not!" she snapped.

"The hell you're not. You're afraid we'll end up making love again. We could, too. Very easily."

"That's enough!" Livid with fury, Kate got to her feet. "I think it's time for you to leave!"

Three

Cooper hadn't arrived with even the vaguest notion of kissing Kate, but all of a sudden kissing her, tasting those rose-petal lips again, was in his mind. He took a long stride and saw Kate back up an equal distance. The look in her eyes contained shock. "Don't you dare."

Like a dash of cold water, her challenge stopped both of them. Her choice of words could have been better, Kate realized uneasily, watching Cooper debate the wisdom of taking the challenge or accepting her renunciation.

Kate couldn't believe that he actually had the audacity to try to incite something physical between them. Yet it was still on his face and in the stance of his body. A strange little bubble of awareness gurgled within her, along with a curling, unnatural heat. Kissing Cooper Sinclair was the last thing she wanted to do in Nevada, but damn him for having the power to make her even think about it!

Cooper shoved his hands into his jeans' pockets and grinned at her. "It's still between us, Katie, like it or not."

She shook her head, refusing to be drawn into his conception of what was going on between them. "You're dead wrong, Cooper. But let me say this. If there *were* still some remnants of that long-ago misbehavior between us, it wouldn't change my purpose here."

He laughed, a rolling, completely masculine laugh. "We could sure have some summer together, Kate."

She recoiled. "Never! I'm not here to have *some summer* with you! And you're not fooling me one bit, either. You're only on this porch for one reason. You're scared spitless over those papers I gave you." At once Kate realized the accusation had been too bold, and she took another step back, not sure just how Cooper would receive it.

What he did was cock an eyebrow and drawl, "Kate, Kate, when did you ever see me scared spitless about anything? Let's just suppose, for the sake of argument, that those documents have some validity. You're an attorney. How many years do you think it would take to fight the whole thing out in court? You and I could both be old and gray before the issue was resolved. First of all, any judge would consider intent. Whether or not old Les actually conveyed those water rights, he *intended* to convey them. Whether or not Sam received them, he *intended* receiving them. If there was an omission in paperwork, it's only a technicality. Sinclairs have possessed the entire valley—other than this hundred acres—*and* the water rights for ten years now. A judge could very well ask, why didn't Les, himself, present a suit to regain control of his water? It's all too obvious why he didn't, Kate. He did nothing because he *thought* he'd signed the rights away with the land.''

Cooper was so convincing, icy fingers curled around Kate's spine. She stared at him during the speech, and then bent over for the glass she'd placed beside her chair and drained the last drops of watery tea from it into her dry mouth. His points were none that she hadn't thought of in New York, however. ''Wait here for a minute,'' she demanded, and hurried into the house.

Her hands were shaking, but by the time she reached the bedroom and retrieved a file folder she'd brought with her, she was relatively collected again. Quickly she sorted through the papers in the folder, and with a small sheaf of them, returned to the porch. ''You may keep these. I have several other copies.''

''What is this?''

''Precedent cases. A list of case numbers, dates, the basis for the litigation and the subsequent rulings. I think you'll find them very interesting.''

Cooper looked down at the papers in his hand and frowned. ''You mean this kind of situation has come before the courts before?''

''Indeed it has. When you show your attorney those documents I gave you earlier, show him that list, too. It will save him a great deal of research time.''

Cooper's eyes narrowed on her. ''You're very sure of yourself about this, aren't you?''

Kate's chin came up. ''Very. I didn't stumble on this just last night, Cooper. I've spent months looking at it from every angle, researching those cases and studying Nevada's water rights statutes. I've talked to people in the state recorder's office in Carson City many times. I've had a title company do a full and thorough study on the history of Mustang Valley, making sure that no subsequent documents regarding water rights were filed after Sam foreclosed on the land. So don't waste your breath threatening me with years of litigation and unsympathetic judges. I would never have come here without understanding my position thoroughly, and I have a solid case, Cooper, a very substantial reason to sue your socks off!"

"Which you'll do," he said dryly.

"Which I most definitely will do. I'm being very fair by giving you until the end of summer to set the record straight."

Cooper folded the papers in half, then again, shaping them to fit into the back pocket of his jeans. "Fair," he echoed tonelessly.

"Yes, fair."

He grinned humorlessly. "I'll bet you just eat those poor New Yorkers alive in court, honey."

Kate flushed, instantly defensive. "I'm a good attorney, Cooper."

"I'm sure you are."

The comment was underlaid with amusement, and Kate's fingernails dug into her palms as her hands clenched. "You're going to find out just how good," she promised in a low voice that was tense with simmering anger.

Cooper turned his back on her and moved to the edge of the porch, pausing at the top of the steps, his glance focused on the ground. "Seems like a hell of a way to spend the summer," he grunted, then took the stairs in two long strides. He whistled for the hound and walked over to his horses.

From the porch Kate watched him swing up into the saddle, then give her a mocking salute by touching the brim of his hat. "You're still so smug, I can't believe it," she whispered. Cooper's visit had shaken her, confident of the legality of her position or not. He'd wanted to kiss her, and she had to wonder why. Her own response to his near attempt still tingled within her, undermining her resolve to cling to old prejudices. He was right about one thing: it was a hell of a way to spend the summer.

Cooper flew the helicopter back to Reno on Tuesday morning as planned. He had Kate's documents with him, and when he passed his secretary's desk on the way to his office, he asked her to set up an appointment with Dave Walker, the attorney who presently handled his legal work.

Then he dove into the countless chores that operating a hotel and casino required on a daily basis. He made the rounds, first spending time in the counting room going over drop records, which were individual tallies of each and every gaming machine on the premises, plus the same kind of information on each table game. The "drop" was the money counted every day. The drop comprised the nickels and quarters and tokens used in the dollar machines that ended up in buckets beneath the machines, and the cash stuffed through special slots into locked boxes on each gaming table.

Sinclair's was a lenient casino, returning a high percentage of coins played in the machines back to the players. Even so, the drop was always good. Winners rarely pocketed their money and left. Casino owners loved winners, and Sinclair's was no exception to that unwritten rule. Substantial winners were "comped," given free dinners and drinks, and most of them played back their win.

After leaving the counting room, Cooper visited the restaurants, kitchens and bars. Then he stopped for a few words with the man who managed the hotel portion of the place. He joked with the bell captain and several cocktail waitresses, pausing to ask after one of the floormen's wives, who'd been in the hospital recently. Then he headed for the accounting department, where he studied more daily reports, these from the "cage."

The cage was the bank of the casino operation. It was where people bought coins, where they cashed checks, where they applied for and received credit, where they cashed in chips won on the craps, twenty-one, baccarat and roulette tables. The cage managed an enormous amount of cash, and there were uniformed and armed security guards watching it at all times. Reports from the cage included the fluctuation of cash and casino chips, and any large payouts to winners. Nothing extraordinary had happened over the weekend during his absence, Cooper saw. He talked to several different accountants about various aspects of their particular duties, then, finally, returned to his own office.

"Dave Walker suggested dinner tonight," Kathy Stover, his secretary, announced as she followed him in. "I told him I'd call him back with your answer."

"Dinner's fine. Only tell him we'll have it in my suite. Around seven." Cooper accepted the stack of telephone messages Kathy handed him and started thumbing through it. "Looks like business as usual," he commented dryly, then gave Kathy a smile. She was a pretty woman, about twenty-two, and madly in love with a young man in medical school. "How's Brian?"

Kathy rolled her eyes dramatically. "Studying his buns off!"

Dave Walker swirled the cognac in his snifter with a concentration that made Cooper uneasy. The attorney had listened all through dinner with few comments. Cooper had presented Kate's papers, but Dave had only given them a cursory glance with a promise to study them later.

Now, with dinner behind them, they were having brandy in the well-appointed study of Cooper's spacious suite. "So, what do you think?" Cooper asked.

Dave shook his head. "I can't give you any kind of intelligent answer tonight, Coop. I need to examine Kate's documents and digest everything you've told me."

"Hell, you don't think she's got any kind of chance, do you?" Cooper pressed.

The attorney frowned, and his changing expression gave Cooper another pang. Dave got up and went over to the low table where he'd left Kate's papers. He shuffled through them a moment, then looked at Cooper. "You know, it's a little out of the ordinary that she gave you so much of her ammunition."

"Did she do that?"

"She did her homework, Coop. I'll check this list of rulings, of course, but I have a hunch that I'll find it's accurate. My point is, *she* feels she's got a case that would hold up in court, and yet she handed over her best arguments. You know, it kind of looks like she'd rather settle this thing peaceably.''

Cooper shook his head and grinned wryly. ''But peaceably to Kate means only one thing, Dave, that I sign over half of Mustang Valley to her.''

''Maybe. But if she doesn't give a damn about the hostility of a court action, why didn't she just breeze into Nevada and file a suit? Hell, she wouldn't even have had to come here to do that. She knows the legal ropes. She could have worked through a Nevada attorney and stayed in New York. Instead she comes to you first. She gives you her research data, the backbone of her case. It kind of looks to me like Kate Redmond doesn't *want* this to come to a court battle.''

The two men exchanged a long look, then Dave asked in a casual tone, ''Any reason you can think of why she might want to avoid that kind of trouble?''

Kisses and intimacy flashed through Cooper's mind, but he tossed off the rest of his brandy and got to his feet with a brusque ''No.''

Dave finished his drink, too, and set the empty snifter on a coaster. ''Well, give me a few days, Coop. If you don't hear from me by the end of the week, give me a call.''

''Thanks, I'll do that.'' Cooper escorted his guest to the door, said good-night, then returned to the study. Splashing a little more cognac into his glass, he sat down again to give the evening some thought.

Did Dave's gut reaction have merit? Did Kate prefer to keep the battle as peaceable as possible? Why *hadn't* she just filed the suit from New York instead of moving into that tumbledown house for the summer? Were there some personal feelings involved in this mess that even she wasn't aware of? And what were his own feelings? He certainly wasn't a man who ordinarily tried to grab a woman and kiss her without some kind of invitation. But that's what he'd done on Kate's porch. Just because he hadn't gone through with it didn't alleviate his intent. They had both known what had been in his mind. In retrospect, Cooper had to question what had come over him, especially when he'd gone over to her place to apologize for virtually the same sin.

Cooper put his head back and pondered the situation. The thought of sharing the valley wasn't that jolting, actually, not if he and Kate were friends. There was ample space, grass and water for twice the number of cattle he was raising, and he had no plans to increase the size of his herd. But he didn't like being pushed, and Kate was pushing hard. Reaching any kind of amicable arrangement didn't look like a simple matter to Cooper.

He'd found himself thinking about Kate a lot since he'd left her on her own porch the other day. She stirred something in him that he couldn't quite lay a finger on. It was like an elusive itch, one he couldn't pinpoint enough to scratch, a disoriented, unsettled feeling that tantalized and teased just on the edge of reason.

Frowning, Cooper shook it off, as he did every time it happened. Kate was trouble, a whole hell of a lot of trouble, and she wasn't entitled to half of Mustang Valley. If it took the rest of his life, he'd fight to protect Sam's memory. That's really what it boiled down to, that old antagonism between Sam Sinclair and Les Redmond. It seemed foolish and a waste of time to Cooper for Sam's and Les's grandkids to be arming themselves for all-out war. But that's where he and

Kate were headed, in spite of his silly urges to kiss her.

And whether the battlefield was a courtroom or dead center of Mustang Valley, there was no way it was going to be peaceable. He and Kate sparked too many emotions in each other to handle this peaceably.

Sinclair barbed wire completely enclosed Kate's hundred acres, and just beyond the fence were hundreds of head of Sinclair cattle and horses. On the other end of the valley, the red-tiled roof of the Sinclair house and the sloping shapes of barns and other outbuildings were all too visible.

Kate was getting used to the continual reminders of Cooper and Sam Sinclair everywhere she looked. She'd known before she ever left New York what she was letting herself in for. She'd steeled herself against the nostalgia awaiting her in Mustang Valley, the memories, both good and bad, of the first eighteen years of her life.

Kate was walking the fence line, plowing through dry grass and weeds. A brisk breeze cooled her face beneath the straw hat she was wearing, and the moister grass on the other side of the fence waved in flowing, rippling patterns. The mountains rimming the valley were purplish on her left and almost gold on her right, a trick of the sun and its position in the sky. The colors changed as the earth moved, and whether the sky was cloudy or clear. On gray days, the mountains could look dark and ominous. On bright, clear days, such as this was, the mountains were gloriously hued.

Some distance from the house, Kate stopped, her gaze directed across the wire fence. Cooper had some magnificent horses, and Kate had found herself watching them with yearning several different times. She wanted a ride, a long, carefree ride through the valley like she'd taken a thousand times in the past. Cooper's cattle meant nothing to her, but his horses did. She longed for a ride. It had been years since she'd been on a horse, which was her own fault, but she'd never been lured by the available riding stables within her reach in New York. It wasn't just sitting in a saddle that drew her like a moth to a flame; it was riding through this valley.

Sighing, Kate started walking again, her thoughts on money. She had two separate savings accounts, her own personal funds and the money Les Redmond had accumulated to pay back the loan he'd gotten from Sam Sinclair. Only Sam had refused to take it, saying it was years overdue and he'd been lenient long enough. He'd wanted Les's land, and he'd taken it. Neither Les nor Kate had ever touched a penny of that money afterward, though there'd been occasions of need, and it had grown with bank interest to an impressive amount.

No matter what else she might want, even a horse, she had determined to keep that old bank account inviolate. It was slated for one thing and one thing only: to pay off that old debt when Cooper signed over Les Redmond's land.

Kate's own funds were limited, and she couldn't afford to spend the entire summer without a salary and buy a horse, too. She'd already used some of her savings for a car, but it was necessary to have transportation in Nevada. Even the nearest grocery store was twenty miles away. It didn't help Kate's mood to realize that the money she'd wasted on that expensive outfit she'd bought to wear when she faced Cooper would buy a pretty decent horse now, and she turned back to the house with a disgusted grimace.

The truth of the matter was that the valley was hauntingly beautiful but lonely. Kate had spotted men on horseback a few times, and one afternoon Leila McCutcheon, Cooper's housekeeper, had dropped in for an hour, bringing along a tin of homemade cookies as a welcoming gift. Kate had been keeping busy enough with getting the house in shape, but she was used to city life now, and the long, silent days and nights were beginning to get her down.

Cooper's extended absence actually stunned her. She should have known that with Sam dead Cooper would be heavily involved with their Reno hotel and casino. But when she'd planned for the summer, she'd consistently depicted the valley with Cooper present, as he'd been before the Redmonds had moved out. In those days it was Sam who ran the Reno business and Cooper had worked on the ranch. The valley seemed strangely empty when Kate looked in the direction of the Sinclair house and remembered that Cooper was in Reno.

She felt ignored, Kate realized, totally and insultingly ignored. Cooper had gone off as though she weren't there threatening a major lawsuit. Didn't it bother him? Wasn't he concerned about it? Didn't he believe she would follow through?

Then it occurred to Kate that Cooper might have declared a war of nerves. The worst part of that conjecture was that it was working, with or without Cooper having planned it. She was on edge, a little more each day, and wanted some kind of hint, at least, as to how Cooper's attorney viewed her documents. Had the man recommended a hard-line stand and whatever

kind of legal battle it took to clear Cooper's ownership? Or had he suggested a sensible, reasonable, out-
of-court settlement?

Kate got bogged down at that point. Les Redmond
had been kicked hard by Sam Sinclair, and would anything less than a deed to the land Sam had greedily
foreclosed on heal that old wound?

It was almost two weeks before Kate heard anything
from Cooper, and then it wasn't a direct contact. A
pickup pulled into her driveway, and Dirk Simons,
Cooper's ranch foreman, got out and came to her front
door.

Kate was glad enough to see *anyone* that she opened
the door with a genuine smile. "Hello, Dirk."

"Hello, Kate. I got a call from Coop. He'd 'uv
called you, but..."

"But I don't have a phone. Come on in, Dirk."

"Thanks." The lanky cowboy stepped over the
threshold and looked around. "Hey, you're really fix-
ing the old place up."

"Doing what I can. May I get you something cold
to drink?"

"Nah, better not. Coop's waiting for a call back. He
wants to send the helicopter for you."

Kate's eyes widened. "The helicopter?"

"He said he's been real busy, but he'd like to talk
to you. He mentioned something about dinner and
staying at the hotel tonight."

Kate turned away, experiencing an odd burst of excitement. Maybe it was only a reaction to the thought
of an evening in Reno, with lights and people and
noise, but it was where Cooper was, too. And they'd
be having dinner together.

She cleared her throat and said speculatively, "Well, I don't know..."

Dirk shifted his feet and tugged at an ear. "Should I tell him you don't wanna go?"

"Well, it's awfully sudden. When would the copter arrive?"

Dirk shrugged. "I guess he'll tell me that if you agree to go."

Of course she was going. Just to see crowds of people, if nothing else. But Kate didn't want Cooper hearing from his foreman that she had leaped on the invitation. "I guess I could be ready in a couple of hours," she sighed, as though the whole thing was just too, too much for her hectic schedule.

"Is that what I should tell him, then?"

Kate hesitated, a dramatic pause, then finally nodded. "Oh, I suppose it won't kill me. I was just getting ready to do some more painting, but it can wait a day. Yes, tell Cooper I'll be ready in two hours."

"Fine." Dirk opened the door and started out.

"I'll drive over when I'm ready," Kate called as the foreman reached his pickup.

"Good enough. See ya then."

Kate closed the door and leaned against it. Her heart was beating unusually hard, and it took a minute for her to realize she shouldn't be so worked up about seeing Cooper tonight. They had serious business to discuss, certainly the only reason he was sending his helicopter for her. He'd had plenty of time to consult with his attorney, and maybe he already understood his weak position and was ready to admit defeat.

But they'd be having dinner together, and she'd be staying in his hotel.

What if he made a pass? What if he tried to kiss

her, as he'd come very close to doing the last time they'd been together? What if he wanted more than a kiss?

Kate drew a sharp breath. "Oh, stop with the wild imagination," she muttered, and pushed away from the door, half angry at her silly meanderings. Even if Cooper tried something, she wasn't going to go along with it. Why was she getting all giddy and female over a business dinner?

In the bedroom Kate stared at her clothes in the small closet. She wanted to look good, but certainly not seductive. She took out a plain black sheath, studied it and finally nodded. After laying it out on the bed, she headed for the shower.

Kate couldn't believe the organization she encountered on the trip from ranch to hotel. The helicopter arrived right on time, a limousine which was waiting for her at the heliport in Reno, whisked her to Sinclair's in very few minutes, and then she was immediately and courteously escorted to a sumptuous suite of rooms.

A basket of fruit with a small, white envelope attached to its handle sat on the bar, which also boasted a bottle of very good champagne in a silver ice bucket. Once the bellboy had deposited her overnight case in the bedroom and gone, and the gentleman who had so pleasantly shown her to the suite had also departed, Kate walked over to the bar and uneasily stared at the gifts.

Perhaps exquisitely perfect fruit and expensive champagne were commonplace items for Sinclair's guests, but they struck Kate as slightly off-key in her case. She really couldn't believe that Cooper was look-

ing forward to tonight's meeting, not unless he had
gotten some very bad advice from his attorney.

With a frown of developing tension, Kate removed
the envelope from the handle of the basket and extracted a card.

Kate,
Please relax or look the place over, whichever
you prefer. I've arranged for dinner in my suite,
number 501 on the fifth floor, at seven.

                                        Cooper

Laying the card and envelope on the bar, Kate went
over to a window. She was on the fourth floor, in suite
number 401, which, if the hotel's rooms were logically
numbered, would be directly below Cooper's. She
moved the curtain aside and looked down to the busy
street. Cars and people and activity held her interest
for a minute, then she dropped the curtain with a sigh.

What had she expected, a personal welcome from
Cooper? She'd arrived hours before the dinner meeting
he'd planned, and he'd been courteous enough to write
a note. She would have to be content with that.

After hanging up the black dress she'd brought for
the evening, Kate checked her appearance in the mirror. She'd worn off-white slacks and blouse for the
helicopter ride, dressing the casual outfit up with some
gold jewelry, a delicate chain around her neck and
earrings. Obviously she hadn't had to bother with jewelry or anything else. Not for Cooper, at any rate.

Kate stared at herself. Had she really dressed for
Cooper?

Turning away, deliberately avoiding the unsettling
question, Kate concentrated on her options for the af-

ternoon. She had no intention of "relaxing," one of Cooper's written suggestions. For one thing she was too keyed up over the evening ahead. But she also wanted to mingle with the crowds she'd seen downstairs. Besides, it had been years since she'd been in Reno, and she'd noticed a lot of changes in the city during the limo ride to the hotel. She would take a nice, long, leisurely walk.

Four

At ten minutes to seven someone knocked on Kate's door. She was ready but hadn't expected Cooper to come for her, and she opened the door with surprise on her face. "Oh. Hello."

"Hello, Kate."

She saw the quick flick of his eyes that took in the black dress, sheer hose and high-heeled black pumps, and immediately understood, from its impersonal haste, that Cooper intended no fast moves tonight. That was fine with her. She was ridiculously nervous as it was, and they certainly had a lot more important things to do than play a sexually oriented game of cat and mouse.

Cooper's smile was reserved, polite. He'd been tied up off and on all day, but he could have made time to greet Kate. It was just better for his long-range plan to have saved everything for this evening. "Sorry I

wasn't downstairs when you arrived. My schedule has
been hectic lately.''

"I understand. There probably aren't enough hours
in the day to keep up with this busy place. I'm all
ready. Just let me get the room key.''

Cooper stood at the open door while Kate went over
to a table where she'd placed the key after her walk.
With her back to him, he took a much more in-depth
look. Her dress was chic, stylishly simple. Tonight, as
with that initial, startling meeting at the Sinclair ranch
house, Kate's New York image was well in place. She
might be a country girl at heart, evidenced by the old
shorts, sneakers and the paint in her hair later that
same day. But, apparently, she was able to slip from
one role to the other with complete ease.

He wasn't condemning the ability. He did the same
thing himself. At Sinclair's he wore business-slanted
clothing. On the ranch he preferred jeans, the older
and more broken-in the better.

"There. All set,'' Kate announced as she dropped
the key into a small black clutch bag. It was on the
way to the elevator that she realized she'd done everything but give Cooper a direct look. She was still
doing it, glancing everywhere but into his eyes. Her
unease annoyed her, adding another facet to the dis-
array of emotions plaguing her.

Cooper pressed the Up button and stood back. "I
hope you didn't find the afternoon boring.''

Kate was staring up at the lighted floor panel above
the elevator doors. "Not at all. I enjoyed walking
around and seeing something of Reno again. It's
changed a great deal since I was last here.''

"You've never been back until now?''

"No.''

A bit of frost had entered Kate's voice, an accusation that her absence was his fault. Cooper darted her a side glance and saw a hint of the stubbornness that had been such a vital part of the younger Kate Redmond's personality. He sighed inwardly. Apparently she was still stubborn.

They stood as far apart as the limited space in the elevator would permit. But it was a short ride, only one floor, so there wasn't time for any real discomfort to develop. Actually, Kate was doing a monumental acting job when, ordinarily, pretense was extremely difficult for her. Her insides were churning sickishly, an affliction that had started—vaguely at first—with Dirk's appearance at her house, and had become increasingly more noticeable all afternoon.

Cooper was too good looking and too much a part of her personal past to pretend this evening was strictly business. It *should* be strictly business, and maybe that's all Cooper saw in it. But Kate was beginning to have some off-the-wall thoughts on the matter. She'd resented the Sinclairs for so long that she'd forgotten how much Cooper had once meant to her. In the past two weeks, along with too much quiet and speculation over what Cooper's attorney might be planning, she'd thought of their last meeting on her porch—particularly that moment when she'd known Cooper had wanted to kiss her—more than she liked.

And going to his suite for a dinner for two really had to be the height of folly. How did two people with their kind of past discuss a possible lawsuit as if it were ordinary business? She had no choice but to go through with the evening now, but why, in heaven's name, hadn't she thought it through a little better before agreeing to a meeting in Cooper's hotel?

Cooper unlocked the door of his suite and pushed it open, standing back to allow Kate to precede him in. A subtle drift of her perfume packed a wallop that he had to forcibly ignore, and there was a strange little frown on his face when he closed the door, then gestured to another doorway. "We'll have a drink in the study. Dinner should be along shortly."

"All right." Cooper's study was an impressive room, Kate saw as she entered. It was very masculine, with fawn-colored leather furniture, a lighted bar, dark wood bookshelves and deep burgundy carpeting. Cooper invited her to sit down, and after a quick survey of her alternatives, Kate settled for the far end of the long leather sofa.

"What can I get you to drink?"

Kate's gaze went to the bar. "A little bourbon and a *lot* of water."

Cooper went around the bar. "Any special brand?"

"No. Anything will do. Frankly, I don't know one brand from another."

"Not much of a drinker, hmm?"

Kate found a smile, albeit one without a whole lot of punch. "Not like our grandfathers, Cooper. I think that was the one area in which they were almost exactly alike, their taste for bourbon." Now why had she even mentioned the word "grandfathers"? Inwardly Kate groaned, seeing the topic as an extremely unpropitious way to begin this meeting.

She felt relieved when Cooper chuckled softly. "And cigars, Kate. Sam loved a good cigar, and as I recall, so did Les." With two cut-glass tumblers, Cooper came around the bar and delivered one to Kate. Then he sat on the chair closest to her end of the sofa. He held up his glass. "Cheers."

"Cheers," she echoed, and took a small sip of her drink. He'd made it light, as she'd requested, and the liquid was cool and went down smoothly. Kate hoped it would settle her nerves. She didn't know just when Cooper would get to the point of the meeting, but she would guard against rushing him, she decided. "I enjoyed seeing the hotel and casino this afternoon."

"I didn't make many changes in the place after Sam died, not in the casino. The hotel rooms needed refurbishing, but that's a never-ending process, anyway." Cooper smiled. "Did you try your luck downstairs?"

"Gamble?" Kate shook her head. "I'm not much of a gambler, I'm afraid."

A teasing twinkle flashed in Cooper's eyes. "She doesn't drink, doesn't gamble. No vices at all, Katie?"

Kate didn't take the bait, but privately winced at the old nickname. "Do *you* gamble?"

Cooper laughed. "I heard the lawyer in you just then, Kate. But no, I don't gamble. Frankly, I don't have a whole lot of respect for gamblers."

The statement startled Kate. "And yet you own and operate a casino. Isn't that a rather conflicting attitude for a casino owner?"

"Maybe. But this is only another business."

"A very lucrative business," Kate commented dryly.

"Do you disapprove?" It was beginning to bother Cooper that Kate kept avoiding eye contact. She looked at her glass, at the bookshelves, at everything and anything but him.

"I really haven't given it any thought," Kate hedged, not wanting to get into a debate on the morality or ethics of operating a business that was perfectly legal but preyed on and profited from people's weaknesses. She felt the weight and burden of Cooper's eyes on her, and took another sip of her drink.

"Why won't you look at me?"

Blinking, Kate shaped a smile and darted him a very brief look. She'd known what he was wearing, of course, gray slacks, a white, open-at-the-neck shirt, and a navy blazer. He was so handsome, her heart skipped two full beats before settling down again. "Sorry," she said quietly, her eyes on her glass again.

"You're uncomfortable."

"Yes."

"Why? You're safe here, Kate."

"It never occurred to me that I might not be." Which wasn't exactly true. Cooper certainly didn't give off any comforting waves of security, not to her, anyway. It was unnerving to remember the confidence she'd felt in New York when she'd envisioned facing Cooper, and she had to wonder where her normal good sense had been. Cooper was a formidable adversary, even if those niggling sensations of awareness would leave her be. As it was, she was much too conscious of his good looks and magnetism to remain detached.

"But you're still uncomfortable."

She didn't like the direction of the conversation. He had to know why she was uncomfortable, and if he wasn't so puffed up with Sinclair smugness, he might have the grace to be uncomfortable, too. "Oh, please," she said with a note of exasperation. "Let's keep this impersonal."

Cooper lifted his glass to his lips, eyeing Kate over the rim while he drank. He'd known and did know many attractive women, but none of them were so interwoven into Sinclair history. Kate was a part of his youth, a part of Mustang Valley. He could see her as she'd been then, untamed, uninhibited, on the back of a horse, with her long hair streaking out behind her. That girl was visible in the present-day Kate, but probably only he had the ability to find her beneath the fine clothes and acquired sophistication.

"We'll talk about something else," he agreed. "How are you coming with the house?"

Kate relaxed against the glove-soft cushions of the sofa. "It's becoming livable. Ten years of dust was its biggest problem."

"It's very outdated." Cooper got up and walked over to the telephone that had interrupted with a melodious ring. "Excuse me," he murmured before picking up the receiver.

While Cooper took care of what was obviously a business call, Kate got up and walked about the room. His last remark, about her house being outdated, didn't bother her too much. One could argue that modern wasn't necessarily best in a house, and she could also let him in on some of the plans she'd been contemplating for the old place's future. Besides, there was meaning in that old house that had nothing to do with style or even convenience. Kate knew, regardless of where else she might hang her hat, that eighteen years had left a lot of ghosts. The spirit of her youth, along with memories of her crusty, outspoken grandfather, roamed those hundred acres. What's more, Les Redmond had built an unusual house for a ranch, and it had—or could have with the right kind of effort—a quaint sort of charm.

At any rate, she could do nothing, other than the painting and cleaning until the suit with Cooper was settled, and Kate didn't see any reason to get into that aspect of their controversy tonight.

Cooper's study was a pleasant room, Kate decided. She hadn't known he was a reader, but the books lining his shelves had been opened and handled, showing signs of indeed having been read. Their subjects were varied, evidencing a taste for history, economics and spy novels. She tried not to listen to Cooper's side of the telephone conversation, but couldn't help noticing his rather terse remarks. Then she heard "I understand. I'll call you later," and the sound of the receiver being put down.

"Sorry about that."

"Quite all right," Kate murmured.

Cooper picked up his glass and finished off the last swallow. "Can I fix you another drink?"

Kate looked down at the glass in her hand and saw that other than two melting ice cubes, it was empty. "No, thank you."

A distinct knocking at the suite's outer door reached the study, and Cooper glanced at his watch. "That will be our dinner. It's right on time." Smiling, he urged Kate from the study with a hand on her back.

"My compliments to your chef," Kate told her host.

They were still at the dining-room table, having coffee. "I'll pass them on," Cooper replied. The food had been excellent, but despite Kate's compliments, she'd eaten little. Cooper took it to mean she still wasn't very comfortable.

They'd talked about a dozen different topics during the meal, each of them studiously avoiding the reason for the meeting. It was time to get to the point. "Let's bring our coffee to the study, Kate," Cooper suggested.

"Fine."

The transition was accomplished quickly, and Kate resumed her previous seat on the sofa. Cooper had been considerate and gentlemanly during dinner, not anything like she had feared, and she was much more relaxed than she'd been earlier. It surprised her that Cooper sat down and sipped coffee without digging around for a cigarette, and she almost complimented him on apparently kicking the habit.

But she was the one who'd asked that the evening be kept impersonal, and Cooper had abided by her request. Scrupulously so, as a matter of fact, which, perversely, annoyed Kate.

She breathed a small sigh, wondering what was wrong with her. It was natural to have some ambivalence where Cooper was concerned, but annoyance at something she'd specifically asked for was totally unreasonable.

Cooper looked at the woman on his sofa. Kate wasn't evading eye contact quite so noticeably now, but neither did their gazes lock for more than a second at a time. Well, they'd eaten together without hostility and it was time to find out just how deep their truce went.

"I'm sure you know my reason for inviting you here," he began.

Kate's gaze flicked up. *Do you have to have such heavenly blue eyes?* Her mouth was suddenly dry, and she swallowed some coffee before answering. "I assume it's because you've talked to your attorney."

"He wanted to be in on this meeting, but I preferred we meet privately."

Not certain where Cooper was heading, Kate remained silent.

"Dave—David Walker—thinks, *hopes,* we can settle this thing out of court."

She cleared her throat. "Did he examine the documents I gave you?"

"Thoroughly."

"And?"

A lengthy pause ensued, and Kate's nerves grew raw with tension. "You have a case," Cooper finally said in a flat, emotionless tone.

A choking jubilation rose in Kate's throat. Was it going to be this easy? Was Cooper admitting defeat?

"But so do I," Cooper announced firmly, and Kate realized her elation had not only been premature, it had been unrealistic. "If you and I don't come to some agreement, Kate, we're in for a hell of a fight. Like I said, Dave hopes we can settle without a court battle. What do you think?"

For the first time all evening Kate didn't retreat from a direct, steady visual exchange. "I would win in court, Cooper."

"Would you? Dave thinks you have a chance, but no more than a fifty-fifty shot. On my side of the ledger is that old, unpaid debt, collected by foreclosure. And Sam's reputation. A hundred solid, substantial businessmen and women would stand up in court and swear that the Sam they'd known wouldn't have deliberately overlooked those water rights. Character witnesses, Kate, people who would attest to Sam's normal business acumen. It was a mistake, Kate, plain and simple. You only have a fifty percent chance of convincing a judge that Les and Sam both knew the water rights weren't conveyed at the time of foreclosure. I have an equal chance of convincing him otherwise."

Kate put her cup down and got up from the sofa. She turned at the bar. "So, you and your attorney have computed our individual chances of winning. Is that kind of thinking due to your line of work?"

"Sarcasm isn't going to help the situation."

Kate studied her own hand for a tense moment, then lifted her eyes with an impatient air. "Where is this conversation going, Cooper? I already gave you my side."

Cooper slowly rose. "Half of the valley? Not tonight, Kate. Talk about this sensibly or prepare to file your suit."

"Sensibly? Perhaps you should give me your interpretation of sensible. Just what, in place of what I demanded, are you offering?"

After a brief glance at his coffee cup, Cooper ignored it and went behind the bar. "Would you like some brandy?"

Kate slid onto one of the barstools. For someone who didn't usually indulge, she'd consumed her share tonight. There'd been wine with dinner and that drink before dinner, and now a little brandy seemed desirable. Kate didn't like the idea of a crutch, but she *was* feeling some strength in this shoot-out, no doubt because of the drinks. "Yes, thank you."

Cooper poured two brandies and set one in front of Kate. Then he picked up the other and came around the bar to occupy the stool next to hers. He wrapped both hands around the snifter and looked down at it. "I'd like to ask you a question."

They were sitting side by side, not touching, not looking at each other. And yet Kate knew she'd never been more aware of a man. What Cooper made her feel was deeply embedded, tied to memory, an irrevocable part of herself. If Cooper didn't feel an invisible but tensile connector between the two of them, Kate would be eternally surprised.

She managed a reasonably calm, "Go ahead. Ask anything you like."

Cooper's voice was low, but compelling. "If our positions were reversed, if you were in my place and I in yours, what would you do?"

Kate froze, with every cell in her body suddenly rigid. "I hardly think *that's* a fair question!"

Turning his head, Cooper looked at her, and Kate felt the impact of his gaze burning into her. "You'd fight me, wouldn't you?" he concluded softly.

Her brain seemed to stall. The question was more than unfair, it was undermining, mind-boggling. "I...might offer you money," she stammered, then flushed as she realized that might sound as though she was really only after money, which was so far from the truth it was laughable. "Please," she added hastily. "Don't misunderstand..."

"No, you're right. Money is the logical answer. What else would I offer you? But that brings us to how much, Kate."

"Just a minute," she mumbled, pressing her fingertips to her temples. She was being railroaded, and yet she didn't want to respond with the anger that was quickly taking shape. A deep breath helped, steadying her voice some. "I'll say this once, Cooper, and hope it makes a lasting impression. I do not want one penny of your money, not one red cent."

"Why not? Is it because settling the issue with money wouldn't bother me all that much?"

He'd hit the target so neatly, Kate recoiled, and the anger she'd been containing began building again. She put one foot down on the floor and started to slide from the high stool. "I think I'd better leave before…" Cooper caught her by the arm, and suddenly they were staring into each other's eyes.

"We haven't settled anything, Kate."

"Did you really think we would?"

"If you didn't, why did you come?"

Good question. *Very* good question. Oh, yes, she thought, vaguely recalling a desire to be with people and activity. What a laugh. What a lie! She was here because of Cooper, because of this man with his thick black hair and handsome, smugly superior face. Because his touch melted her bones, and just being in the same room with him brought everything female in her to life.

He clung to her arm, with his face only inches from hers. "I have a plan, a suggestion," he said softly. "I knew we'd come to an impasse. We're a lot alike, Kate, both stubborn, headstrong people. If you would have agreed to *anything* I offered, I probably wouldn't have believed it."

Her lips barely moved and her voice was a husky whisper. "What plan?" Was he going to attempt a kiss again?

"You're going to be here all summer. You gave me until the end of summer, right?"

"Yes."

"I'm going to take it, Kate, the entire summer. On Labor Day, we'll talk about this again."

"What?" Kate wrenched her arm free and put some space between them. "What are you talking about?" she spat.

"Are you reneging on the time?"

"No, but I didn't mean for you to mull and ponder…"

"I don't plan to mull and ponder. In fact, I don't intend to even think about those documents the rest of the summer. Labor Day, Kate. On Labor Day I'll either give you what you want or we'll go to war."

Suspicion filled her mind. "Just what are you up to?"

Cooper's hands rose, palms up, a placating gesture. "I'm up to nothing, except anticipation of a peaceful summer. Enjoy the summer, Kate. Enjoy the valley. I get to the ranch little enough, and that's sure what I plan to do when I'm there."

"You're hoping I'll change my mind," she accused heatedly. "I won't."

"Maybe, maybe not. But you have the same possibility with me. Maybe by Labor Day I'll be happy to sign over half the valley to you without a whimper."

Her hand nervously rose to her throat. "I don't trust you."

His face hardened. "I'm not a liar. You might have reason to dislike me, but it's not because I ever lied to you. I won't do anything further on the water rights issue this summer, nor will my attorneys."

Kate's heart was jumping around like a drop of water on a hot skillet. When she'd decided to give Cooper the summer, she'd envisioned… What? she wondered. Meetings between the two of them? Discussions? She felt suddenly drained, oddly empty. She'd seen the two of them in the valley, not in a hotel room in Reno with Cooper holding the best hand. How had this happened? "I…I don't know. I'm not really sure what you're suggesting. This is a serious matter. How can either of us just forget it for two months?''

She chewed her bottom lip for a moment. ''I shouldn't be speaking for you. Maybe you wouldn't have any trouble putting it aside. But I can't see myself pretending I'm in Nevada for a vacation.''

He smiled generously. ''Why not? You're here, with almost the whole summer ahead. Can't you relax and enjoy it? You used to know how to relax. I remember coming up on you one day when you were lying in the grass and watching clouds. Do you remember that?''

Kate turned away. ''No,'' she lied, not wanting to start a round of who remembered what of those years.

''And riding? You loved riding, Kate. To this day I haven't met another woman who handles a horse as well as you.''

''Yes, well… It takes a horse to go riding, and…'' Oh, hell, she thought disgustedly. Her financial situation was none of Cooper's business, and the last thing she wanted was to make a bid for his sympathy. ''I have too much to do in the house to be traipsing all over the valley on a horse.''

Speculation entered Cooper's expression, but Kate wasn't looking at him and missed it. He took a sip of brandy. ''Maybe we've talked about this enough for tonight. You'd probably like to give it some thought.''

Kate was frowning. ''It appears I tied my own hands by giving you the summer.''

Cooper got to his feet. ''Why *did* you give me the summer, Kate?''

Her thoughts became jumbled again. ''Because…I thought…''

''Thought what?''

"Well, I knew it would be a shock to you, and that you'd need time to understand the authenticity of my position, I suppose. Oh, it doesn't really matter, does it? It obviously was a mistake."

"Not a mistake, a kindness."

"No! Whatever you do, don't look at it as a kindness." Cooper had moved closer, and Kate began to anxiously look around. "Where did I put my bag?" She felt his fingertips graze her hair, and ducked her head in the opposite direction. "Please don't do that."

"You have beautiful hair, Kate. It's a little more tamed than it used to be, but it still looks like sunbeams through honey."

There was something in his voice. She'd known he wouldn't keep this entirely impersonal, and oddly, instead of anger, she felt relief. From the moment he'd appeared at her door she'd both applauded and taken exception at his restraint, an ambiguous attitude that had puzzled her all evening.

She stared into his eyes, and knew why she'd been avoiding them. They contained power and confidence and a masculinity that made her shiver. Deep, dark blue irises with black pupils, black lashes, tiny lines at their outer corners that hadn't been there ten years ago. Eyes were the corridor to a person's soul, and for a moment Kate looked directly into emotion.

But then it was gone, and he spoke quietly. "What time would you like the helicopter available in the morning?"

The tight band around her chest made breathing difficult. She moved away and picked up her handbag. "Early."

"Give me a time."

"Eight."

"Fine. I'll make the arrangements."

Kate edged toward the door. "Thank you for dinner."

"I'll see you to your suite."

"That's really not necessary."

She may as well have saved the objection. Cooper opened the suite's outer door for her and then followed her out. They waited for the elevator. "I'll be at the ranch right after the Fourth of July holiday."

The long holiday weekend was almost a week away. "I would imagine it will be a busy weekend for you," she said dully, experiencing a stinging loneliness. The summer had lost import. Labor Day was two months away. Perhaps she should return to New York.

"The Fourth is always busy. I'll be glad for a few days in the valley when it's over."

The elevator doors opened and they stepped into the car. Cooper pressed the fourth floor button. Kate leaned against the back wall. "I'll be going on downstairs for an hour or so. Maybe you'd like to come along," she heard.

"Business?"

Cooper nodded. "You could get a behind-the-scenes view of the place, if you're interested."

Kate thought about it. Following Cooper around while he took care of business wasn't an appealing prospect. "No, I think not. Thank you, anyway."

The elevator stopped, and they got off and walked to Kate's suite. She had her key ready and inserted it into the lock. "Well, I'm not sure what we accomplished, but I appreciate the effort."

"Look at me, Kate."

She turned her face to him, looking up. His height was at least six inches greater than hers, even with her high heels. He wasn't the Cooper she remembered; he was a handsome, well-groomed businessman. The younger Cooper had been rugged and rough around the edges. The ten years had changed them both dramatically, and Kate wasn't all that sure the changes were for the better.

He touched her cheek, and she let him. "Can't we be friends?" he asked softly.

"Is that what you want, friendship?"

He nodded. "Yes, very much. Like we used to have."

She realized he remembered the past differently than she did. Her response was an honest, "I don't know, Cooper. Maybe."

"Think about it. I'll come by and see you after the Fourth." His fingers drifted down her cheek, then followed the gentle curve of her throat. His touch burned her skin, speeding up her pulse beat, knotting her stomach.

"Good night," she said quickly, and turned the key in the lock. After she was inside with the door closed, she looked through the peephole. He stood there for a long moment with a thoughtful, almost pensive expression, then turned and walked back to the elevator.

Five

Kate got back to her house just before eleven the next morning. She changed to jeans and sneakers and went out to one of the old storage buildings. The tools and equipment her grandfather had left behind were dirty and rusty, but she dug out a rake and a hoe and attacked the mammoth weeds in the yard around the house with a vengeance.

Kate was seething, and she wielded the hoe and cold-heartedly murdered one weed after another. Very much as she'd like to do to Cooper Sinclair. For most of the night she'd replayed their little chat, and it had grown more apparent by the hour that she'd been had. How cleverly he'd taken advantage of her generous time limit! She should have struck silently, without warning. She should have stayed in New York, hired a Nevada attorney and filed her suit! She should have...

As usual, hindsight was twenty-twenty.

Why had she felt so strongly about talking to Cooper before she did anything legally, damn it, why? Now *he* felt completely justified in pushing her right up to her own deadline.

Wiping her sweating forehead on her shirt sleeve, Kate leaned on the hoe. Her gaze drifted over Cooper's cattle and horses, beyond the vast green fields, clumps of trees and familiar terrain to Cooper's house. Or, the roof of his house, which was really all she could see from her place. For a few minutes she stared, with anger, with resentment, and then gradually realized that someone, on horseback, was coming her way.

She watched, much as she had the afternoon Cooper had ridden over, and realized very quickly that this rider wasn't him. Which, of course, she'd known beforehand. Cooper was in Reno.

Recognizing Dirk Simons after a bit, Kate hacked at another weed, her thoughts back on Cooper's treachery. The man wasn't to be trusted. Which should be no big surprise, she told herself with acute, self-directed criticism. He'd seen and used the one aspect of her stand that she hadn't anticipated, and she definitely *should* have anticipated it.

All summer, indeed! What was the point of hanging around here all summer if…?

"Kate?"

She turned and shaded her eyes with a hand. Dirk was just outside the barbed-wire fence, and Kate frowned. He had *two* horses, the one he was riding and another he was leading, which she hadn't seen when he'd been a further distance away. "Hello, Dirk," she called, and brought the hoe and rake over to the house to lean them against the weathered shake siding.

Then she started for the fence. Dirk had dismounted and was opening the stock gate. "I've got something for you," he said with a big grin.

Kate's gaze moved to the second horse, and she realized Cooper had caught her slip last night. Her first impulse was an urge to utter a firm, "No way. Take him back, Dirk. I don't want or need any Sinclair charity." But then she took a good look at the horse. He was saddled and a magnificent animal, big, muscular, graceful, and the most incredible blue gray color she'd ever seen.

She moved close enough to touch him. "He's spectacular," she said huskily, instantly emotionally drawn to the animal. Stroking the horse's nose and long, arching neck, she asked, "What's his name?"

"Shadow. Coop said to bring him over for you to ride. You can turn him out in that pasture—" Dirk gestured at the closest field "—when you're not riding him, and I'll also bring over some hay and oats later."

Kate wanted to refuse. She knew she *should* refuse. She also knew she was rationalizing, telling herself that there was really nothing wrong with a rancher loaning a neighbor a horse. And, heaven help her, she wanted to leap onto Shadow's saddle and take a ride so badly she ached.

"Shadow," she murmured softly. "You're a real beauty, aren't you?" His hide was like blue gray velvet, and she couldn't stop petting and caressing the beautiful animal.

"He's one of Cooper's favorites," Dirk said proudly, stroking Shadow's flank.

"I can readily see why. Well, this is very...

neighborly of Cooper,'' she finally allowed. ''All right. The next time you talk to him, tell him thank you for me. I'll take very good care of Shadow.''

''I'll do that, Kate.'' Dirk swung up into the saddle again, nodded and rode off.

Kate latched the stock gate behind him, then turned back to the elegant horse left behind. ''Now, let's you and I get acquainted, my friend,'' she said with a lilt in her voice.

The week went quickly. Kate rode every day, ignoring the strain of muscles she hadn't used for so long. She explored the valley the way she'd been longing to, visiting long-remembered, favorite spots. She rode Sinclair land freely, knowing full well that Cooper hadn't loaned her a horse with the expectation of her staying on her own hundred acres.

It was two days after the Fourth that Kate spotted the helicopter flying into the valley. She was riding Shadow near a bend in the river, and the blue and white copter flew right over her head. Kate watched it zoom by, then stared after it with a tug of emotion. Cooper was coming home.

For a moment Kate was still, and then she turned Shadow's head toward her own place. The thought of Cooper back in the valley made her heart beat faster, and she questioned the reaction, finally admitting that Cooper inhabited a space in her consciousness that nothing or no one else had ever been able to dislodge.

When she and Les left the valley, they'd first moved to Montana, then on to Virginia. Les had gotten employment on a horse ranch, and they'd struggled through Kate's education. They'd rarely spoken of Nevada, and certainly never of the money lying in the bank. For years it was as if that savings account didn't exist, as if it were tainted money.

Les Redmond hadn't died an unhappy man. He'd made some sort of peace with his lot in life, and in actuality, Kate fostered much more bitterness toward the Sinclairs than her grandfather had. But she was clearheaded enough to realize that her and Cooper's personal involvement had greatly influenced her feelings about the foreclosure of Redmond land.

It was still influencing her. Kate rode with a frown, her hands in automatic control of the reins. Just knowing that Cooper was back in the valley was disturbingly satisfying. Her mood had taken a decided upswing after Dirk had delivered Shadow, but she knew she'd been waiting all the same. Waiting for Cooper.

Kate drew a ragged breath. She'd never even come close to admitting such a thing before, but she found herself facing the possibility of deep, immutable feelings for Cooper. For ten years she'd labeled every emotion memory had evoked as resentment. Now she was beginning to wonder. Resentment didn't make one's palms sweaty, or excite one's heart to nervous palpitations, did it?

Upon reaching her own hundred acres, Kate unsaddled Shadow and turned him into the pasture. She went inside, took a shower, dried and curled her hair and dressed in a gold and green print sundress. Also, she applied a little makeup, which she hadn't done in days.

Then she sat on the porch with a glass of iced tea and stared at the distant Sinclair rooftop. He would come. Kate would be willing to bet almost anything that Cooper would be along.

* * *

Cooper had seen Kate from the helicopter. The sight of her on Shadow, her back straight, her jeans' clad thighs curved around the saddle, had nudged old memories. He spent a few minutes with Dirk, then changed into ancient, comfortable jeans and boots. He was riding Monty, on his way to Kate's house within the hour.

He'd told Dave Walker about his plan, and while the attorney hadn't completely agreed that ignoring the potential lawsuit all summer was the best course, he had agreed that friendship with Kate couldn't hurt.

Friendship. Was that all he wanted from Kate? It was a question Cooper had mulled over again and again during the week. Friendship. That's what they'd had before that night ten years ago. Was it possible to go back to friendship with that wild night between them? And if all he wanted was friendship, why was he rushing to see her so soon? He'd be here for three days, plenty of time for a casual, drop-in visit.

Cooper felt his blood stirring. It was crazy, but ever since Kate's evening in Reno, he'd had trouble with his damned libido. Crazier still was that he hadn't been able to direct it to another woman. And it seemed almost insane that he'd had Kate in his hotel, his territory, and hadn't felt so driven. Of course, he'd determined before she'd arrived to keep things cool between them.

It was still the wisest course. How could he keep forgetting what kind of hell was in her power to raise? Yeah, friendship. That's all he wanted from Kate Redmond, a nice, friendly summer, and by Labor Day they'd both be ready to communicate about the water rights issue on a sensible basis.

Cooper spotted Kate on the porch, and as Monty

clip-clopped along and brought him closer, he saw that she was wearing a dress. She'd changed clothes and appeared to be waiting. Cooper's blood raced; Kate was waiting for him.

From the saddle he unlatched the stock gate, then directed Monty through the opening. Again from the saddle, he rehooked the catch, and he didn't dismount until the big black horse stood right at the foot of Kate's porch. "Hi," he said as he climbed the stairs.

"Hello, Cooper."

She remained in the chair, appearing calm and controlled. Cooper took his hat off and sat on the porch railing. "Warm today."

"It's been quite warm for the last *few* days."

His gaze moved over her. Her arms and shoulders were tanner than the last time he'd seen her. Inch-wide straps over her shoulders supported her dress, and he was positive she wasn't wearing a bra. The younger Kate had never bothered with brassieres, and her firm little nipples poking bumps into whatever old shirt she'd worn had bothered Cooper on more than one occasion.

"Thank you for loaning Shadow to me."

"You're welcome." Cooper smiled. "Been exploring the valley?"

"At great length. I've trespassed, of course."

A slight chill in the admission, which Cooper caught and understood to mean that much of the land she'd ridden had once belonged to her grandfather, tinged the atmosphere for a moment. But neither expanded on it.

Kate stood up. "Would you like a glass of tea?"

"Yes, thanks." Cooper got up and leaned against a post while Kate was gone. The peaceful scene of graz-

ing animals and distant mountains beyond Kate's
fence line calmed his soul, as the valley always did.
He'd done some traveling, but nothing he'd seen in
Europe or the Orient had given him the sense of contentment Mustang Valley did.

"Here you are." Turning, Cooper took the glass
Kate was holding out, and their fingers brushed briefly
during the exchange.

"Thanks." Cooper swallowed half of his drink.
"That's good tea." He eyed the extra chair on the
porch, the one that hadn't been there on his first visit.

"Sit down," Kate invited.

"Thanks." He sat and stretched his long legs out
in front of him. "It's nice here. How are you coming
with the house?"

"It's clean now," Kate replied simply.

"I see you're doing some work in the yard, too."
A sprinkler was spraying an oscillating arc of water
on grass that was beginning to green up. The weeds
had been dug out, which had left some patches of bare
earth, but the place was looking much better.

"Yes, the yard was in bad shape. I saw your helicopter coming in."

Cooper turned his head and gave her a long look.
"I saw you, too. Riding Shadow near the river."

Kate felt oddly choked. They'd been speaking so
formally, as if each were afraid to cross a line. She
wanted to say something preposterous, something that
would relieve the stilted atmosphere. The sad truth
was, everything she thought of was either about the
pending lawsuit or the two of them, both subjects to
steer clear of.

A playful breeze came out of nowhere and lifted
Kate's skirt. She slapped it down immediately, but not

before Cooper got a glimpse of a long, smoothly skinned thigh. A burst of desire struck him, and he had to clear his suddenly clogged throat. Kate darted him a glance as the unexpected moment brought their formality down to earth with a crash. Their eyes met, and then tentative smiles turned to laughter.

If felt good to laugh, the first they'd shared. Kate sipped some tea, decidedly more at ease. "Did you have the busy Fourth you anticipated?" she asked.

"Incredibly busy. People by the thousands."

"You're certainly not complaining."

"Not about profits. But the rest of it? To be perfectly honest, I wonder why I keep doing it."

Her eyes widened. "Operate Sinclair's? It never occurred to me that you might not be completely enthralled with the place."

"Sam was enthralled with the place. It's only a business to me, and I don't mind telling you it's been diminishing in appeal for a long time." Cooper gestured broadly. "This is what *I'm* enthralled with. I love this valley." He looked at Kate. "Do you love it, Kate?"

Her eyes narrowed on the surrounding scenery. "I used to. Now it's rather lonely. I didn't expect it to be."

Cooper kept watching her. "If you could, would you live here permanently?"

"I..." Kate stopped herself. Before she'd left New York she had thought she could be happy in Mustang Valley for the rest of her life. Now she honestly didn't know. But that sort of ambivalence could influence Cooper much too much. She had a feeling that if he thought she might not personally use the land she would gain from the lawsuit, he would fight her tooth and nail, ad infinitum. And she'd been thinking of that small chance that he might, as he'd said that night in Reno, "just sign over half of the valley without a whimper."

That, of course, would be the most desirable conclusion to her quest here. It was also, in utter reality, the most unlikely, but that slim chance did have a certain drawing power. Kate wasn't a comfortable liar, but she took a breath and replied, smoothly enough, "Yes, I would live here permanently."

"What about your career?"

"I'd probably take the Nevada bar exam. I could practice law and still live right here, just as you run Sinclair's and call the valley home."

Studying her another moment, Cooper finally nodded. "Yes, I guess you could." He finished the tea in his glass, then stood up. "Would you come over to the house for dinner tonight?"

Kate's stomach began that old familiar churning, and she rose slowly. "Cooper..." she began with protest in her voice.

"It's just a neighborly invitation, Kate. Leila's frying up a bunch of chicken and putting together one of her great potato salads. She and Dirk will be eating with us."

"Oh."

He grinned and touched the tip of her nose with his forefinger. "It's no big deal, Kate. Just a pleasant dinner among friends."

And just like that, with a contact that should have been only innocuous, everything simple between them changed. Kate sucked in a sharp breath and Cooper's smile vanished. Resting on the path of their locked gazes were memories and emotions, both old and new.

Their isolation was suddenly meaningful, as was his maleness, her femaleness. The years of their youth were in the air, dominated by that one night, so strong and real it was almost tangible.

They both backed up a step, with Cooper looking off, his expression taut. Battling the pounding of her heart, Kate brought a hand to the bare skin between the straps of her dress, just below her throat. She found a reasonable facsimile of her normal voice. "Thank you for the invitation, but no."

"Kate, I'm not trying to press you into anything," he said hoarsely, still not looking at her.

She didn't believe him, but she pretended to. "It's not that, Cooper. I just remembered that I already have dinner cooking." Which wasn't a lie, but a simmering pot of vegetable beef stew didn't have to be eaten the day it was prepared.

He knew it was no use; she'd become wary about the intensity of a casual touch. He couldn't blame her; it had startled him, too. "Some other time, then."

"Yes, some other time," she echoed, and heard the false note in her voice.

Cooper heard it, too, and something rather hopeless entered his voice. "Well, guess I'll be heading back."

"Nice of you to come by."

After descending the stairs, Cooper picked up Monty's reins and looked up at Kate. "I'd like us to take a ride together. How about tomorrow morning?"

An unexpected thrill shot through Kate. Take a ride together like they'd done so many times in the past? They'd done a lot of silly things, like breaking into a wild race on the spur of the moment, or going swimming in the river with their clothes on. One time they'd ridden their horses right into the river, and cooled the animals off along with themselves.

She could keep Cooper at bay—except for this. She could refuse dinner invitations and back away from even a hint of a pass, but the desire to ride with him was stronger than common sense.

"I'd love to take a ride in the morning," she said, and watched a light turn on in Cooper's eyes. Her acceptance was important to him, she realized, and felt a special communion with him at that moment.

He swung up into the saddle and smiled. "See you about seven."

Kate nodded. "I'll be ready."

The house was warm and stuffy that evening, and Kate again sat on the porch. It was an incredibly beautiful night with a velvety sky full of stars and air that felt like silk against her skin. The quiet of the valley was broken only by sounds from the pastures and an occasional far-off barking, no doubt from the Sinclair hounds.

Kate felt as far away from New York City as one could possibly get, if not in miles, certainly in ambiance. To avoid attracting nocturnal insects, she sat in the dark, and only a small light from the kitchen shone anywhere on the Redmond acreage.

She heard a motor noise minutes before she saw the vehicle's headlights, and then quickly got up from the chair when it turned into her driveway. Kate leaned over the railing to see who was paying her a visit, and realized that the tall form getting out of the pickup could only be Cooper's. He was carrying something.

"You weren't in bed, were you?" he called, walking toward her.

"No. The house is warm. I've been sitting on the porch."

Cooper reached the stairs. "Leila sent this over."

Kate caught the aroma of chicken from beneath the napkin wrapped around a plate. "Leila?" she said wryly.

Cooper laughed. "All right, me. I thought you might enjoy some of the best fried chicken in Nevada."

Shaking her head in bemusement, Kate accepted the plate. "Thank you. I know I'll enjoy it. Thank Leila for me, even if it was your idea. I'll put this in the refrigerator." At the door she called, "Would you like a beer or something?"

"Sure, sounds good."

Kate brought out two icy cans of beer and handed one to Cooper. She was about to sit down when he said, "Let's take a little walk."

Shrugging, Kate followed him off the porch. She couldn't imagine why he'd come back tonight when they were going riding in the morning, but bringing the fried chicken had been thoughtful. They were away from the house before either spoke. "I'm drawn to you, Kate," Cooper said quietly.

She felt the words, almost like an electrical shock. They kept on walking, drawing nearer to the strands of barbed wire, but Kate's steps were suddenly awkward.

"Dinner was good, and then I watched the news on TV. All the time I kept thinking about you."

She couldn't allow this, she thought. There was too much bad blood between them for this. Her voice was low. "Don't, Cooper."

"Thinking of someone isn't a crime, Kate." He

laughed sharply. "Why am I thinking of you so much? God knows, I'm not trying to."

"I wouldn't know," she said coolly, not particularly flattered by his tone. "Of course, I did burst back into your life rather suddenly."

"I'm not thinking of you in that context."

Kate stopped walking. "Then, in what context, Cooper?"

"Don't put those icicles in your voice, Kate."

"What would you like in my voice?"

"Not icicles. Come on, walk with me." Cooper took her arm, and didn't let it go when they started walking again. Kate felt his thigh moving in rhythm with hers and the hard bulk of his body against her side. "I'm not pressuring you," he said.

"That could be debatable," she replied dryly, so aware of his scent and aura she was getting dizzy.

"I'm *not*," he insisted. "Why would I when I don't even understand why you're haunting me?"

Kate grimaced. "You really know how to make a woman feel great, don't you? *Haunting* you?"

"You know what I meant, and it wasn't anything derogatory."

They stopped at the fence, and Kate extricated herself from his hold, her gaze on the dark animal shapes in the pasture. "You baffle me, Cooper," she said quietly.

"Well, you baffle me, too. You want to know something funny? You always did. When I came around here I never knew if you were going to light into me about something or be glad to see me." He chuckled softly. "What a mouth you had. Not only could you outride most men, you could outswear them."

"Granddad should have washed my mouth out with

soap," Kate said with a short laugh. She sighed then. "I miss him, Cooper. How about you? Do you miss Sam?"

"A lot. Every once in a while I forget he's gone. I'll be doing something and think, 'I'll have to tell Sam about this.' And then I remember. I know he had his faults, but he was mother, father and both grandparents, all rolled into one, for me. You and Les were the same, Kate. You know what I'm talking about."

"Yes," she agreed softly. "Kind of odd how we both…"

"We're a lot alike."

"Well, I don't know if I'd go that far, but our backgrounds are very similar."

Cooper turned and looked down on her in the dark. "Maybe that's the draw, Kate. You stirred up history by coming back here." He reached out and slid his hand beneath her hair, lightly caressing the back of her neck. "There's more to it than that, though, isn't there?"

Goose bumps had popped out all over Kate's skin because of the big hand under her hair. "There's more," she agreed quietly. "But it's only physical, Cooper."

"*Only* physical?" Through reflected starlight they gazed into each other's eyes. Cooper drew back first, with a sighed, "Yeah, you're right. It's this great night making me think crazy thoughts. Well, I better go and let you get to bed. The house has probably cooled off by now."

"Probably," Kate murmured, refusing to heed the urge to gulp air. She could deal with her breathlessness once he was gone.

They walked back to the porch. "See you in the

morning," Cooper said as he continued on to his pickup.

"Good night." Slowly Kate sank back onto her chair. The sound of the pickup disappeared, but she didn't get up and go inside. For a long time she sat and listened to the chirps of insects, pondering the risk she'd taken in coming back to Mustang Valley, a risk that had nothing to do with lawsuits.

Six

Up early, Kate was ready and waiting when Cooper, riding Monty, arrived at seven. Shadow had been saddled and waited in the shade of the house, although the morning was pleasantly cool.

"Good morning," Cooper called brightly when Kate came out of the house.

"It's a glorious morning," she returned cheerfully, and draped the leather thong of her canteen of water around Shadow's saddlehorn.

Their apparel was so similar they could have been twins. Old, faded jeans, boots, pale blue chambray shirts and battered hats. Cooper wore mirrored sunglasses; Kate's were dark-lensed. There was excitement in the air, as if they were about to embark on some great adventure, and Kate wondered if Cooper felt it as strongly as she did.

Kate mounted quickly and they set out. The horses

were fresh and full of vinegar, prancing in the clear morning coolness. "Which way?" Kate asked as Cooper latched the stock gate behind them.

"I've been thinking about Coyote Creek. Does that suit you?"

"Coyote Creek sounds great. I haven't been there yet." Kate spotted two red hounds running across the field toward them and laughed. "Looks like your friends caught up with you."

"Looks like it. Stop that damned yapping," he yelled at the two eager dogs. Then, glancing at Kate, he laughed. His teeth were white and his skin dark, and Kate laughed, too, but not without noticing how utterly beautiful he was. "Beautiful" as in perfection, as in an exquisite balance of masculine features and musculature. Dressed as he was, astride a horse, he was the Cooper of her youth. And what remained of youth in Kate Redmond still loved him.

Stricken by an awakening of knowledge, Kate held Shadow back, giving Cooper the lead and herself a chance to recover. She felt as though she'd just suffered a body blow, and wondered how she could be so disloyal as to love an enemy. Not just love him, but be *in* love with him. Surely she hadn't used the water rights issue just to see Cooper again?

No, that theory was unfair to herself. She could have come back anytime. The hundred acres and house belonged to her, and she could have vacationed in the valley, or even moved back at any time. In fact, if her motive in returning had been strictly Cooper, they would have had a much better chance of getting along without the threat of a lawsuit between them.

The honest to God's truth was, she hadn't realized how she felt toward him. But now so much of the past ten years made sense, her inability to really fall in love with the men she'd admired, her reluctance to seriously commit to anyone. At eighteen she'd been truly, deeply in love with Cooper, and anger and frustration and distance had only disguised the emotion, not eradicated or destroyed it.

It was a thundering comprehension, and sick at heart, Kate concealed it behind an impassive mask. Traditionally they hadn't talked much during rides, and today she was glad. One or the other of them would point out a jackrabbit or a circling hawk, and after comments, they would fall back into a comfortable silence. Kate wasn't so comfortable today, but she made the normal responses when Cooper let her know that a snake was snoozing on a sun-baked boulder he was passing, and a little later called her attention to a herd of antelope in the distance.

Why today? she asked herself. Why, like a bolt out of the blue, had she suddenly been blasted by a recognition of feelings that could only hurt her? Already she felt the pinch of remembering Cooper's cavalier on-again, off-again friendship, how he'd only had time for Katie Redmond in between hell-raising escapades with his countless girlfriends.

Just last night he'd said, "I'm drawn to you, Kate." Which meant, unless he'd changed a heck of a lot, that he was in an on-again mood, and that there wasn't someone more interesting in his life at present. Kate knew she had no confidence where Cooper was concerned, and she wasn't foolish enough to take anything he might say in a good mood as serious.

"I'm drawn to you" could mean a dozen different things, from a desire to take her to bed to this almost ritualistic horseback ride. Even last night she hadn't allowed herself to read anything important in Cooper coming back with the fried chicken and talking in such a vein. Now, with her feelings so exposed and vulnerable, if only to herself, Kate knew she'd have to be doubly on guard. The risk she'd recognized last night had increased to staggering proportions now.

There was both familiarity and discovery in the ride. The landscape had changed little beyond a normal ten-year maturation, and yet the valley, which Kate had already learned from her solitary forays the past week, felt differently than it used to. She'd been hoping, she realized, that riding with Cooper would give her what she remembered so well, contentment, satisfaction, the exuberance she'd once taken so much for granted that she'd never given it a thought.

It wasn't happening. She felt like an outsider. One with a treasure trove of memories, to be true, but while the valley had remained virtually the same, she had changed. And there was no way to regain even the erratic relationship she and Cooper used to have. He might be able to forget the reason she was in Mustang Valley for the summer, but Kate knew it wouldn't leave her mind for a minute.

"Getting tired?" Cooper had turned in the saddle and was looking back.

Kate shook her head. "Not a bit. Are you?"

He grinned and faced forward again, and it was another hour before either of them spoke again.

They reached the spot where Coyote Creek emptied into the river close to noon. They'd climbed some, leaving the valley floor to ascend a series of softly rolling foothills. They were still far below the tree line, and the hills boasted a spindly evergreen only now and again. Coyote Creek was almost hidden in vegetation, however, with sycamores, cottonwoods, elms and small pines thickly interspersed with a variety of low-growing bushes. Cooper led them to the same little clearing they'd visited many times in the past, and by then Kate was glad to get out of the saddle.

On the ground, she stretched her back with a muffled groan. The two horses eagerly dipped their muzzles into the clear creek water, and Cooper walked around and looked the place over. "I haven't been here in a long time."

"No?" Kate eyed him with the weight of her new knowledge. Cooper always had moved with unusual grace for a man his size. She watched him as he prowled the clearing, standing with her hands pressed into the ache in the small of her back. He had great legs, long and straight and filling out his jeans. And a great behind, too. Still no signs of flab around his middle, either.

Unhappy with what she was doing, Kate took her sunglasses off and forced her gaze in another direction.

They drank from their canteens, then Cooper went over to his horse and lifted the flap on one of his saddlebags. Grinning, he brought out two paper-wrapped sandwiches and handed her one.

"Looks like you thought of everything," Kate remarked dryly, accepting the sandwich.

Cooper tucked his sunglasses into a saddlebag and walked around while he ate. Kate sat down in the shade of a tall cottonwood. The long ride had taken its toll; she had aches where she hadn't even known she had muscles. "I guess I forgot how far away this place is," she remarked.

"You're tired."

"Not so tired as stiff. Aren't you? Are you used to that kind of ride?"

"I do a lot of running."

That explained his still lean physique.

He wandered over and plopped down on the grass beside her, his back against the tree, one long leg stretched out, the other knee bent, and finished his sandwich. It took Kate another few minutes to do away with hers, then she took off her hat, bunched it up for a pillow and laid down with a sigh.

Looking up, the mixture of green leaves and pine needles all but blocked the sky. It was cool and peaceful and she could hear the creek gurgling and splashing along. Out of the corner of her eye she could also see a long, firm mound of faded denim, Cooper's hip and leg, barely six inches away.

"Isn't this great?"

His voice had been hushed, as if he didn't want to shatter the stillness. In Kate's mind were some of their other visits to this spot, and she smiled.

"What are you thinking about?" he asked.

Her hands were resting on her stomach, her eyes still on the patches of blue she could see through the foliage. "About the time you went into the woods and pretended to be a bear."

Cooper's laugh echoed through the clearing. "It worked. You ran like a burnt goose."

"Only for a minute," she protested mildly.

"You sure were cute, running and squealing."

Kate's head turned, and she sent him another protest. "I *never* squealed."

Cooper's laughter rang out again. "You're right. You cussed. Damn, you could cuss." He scooted down away from the tree, lying on his side, his head supported by an elbow, looking down on her. Kate saw then that his expression had grown serious, and her stomach suddenly knotted. "Katie, what happened that night? Do you ever wonder about it?"

She didn't have to touch him to feel him, Kate acknowledged. Not that she couldn't if she wanted to. He was very close, close enough for her to see the fine pores in his skin, the sheen of dark whiskers just below the smooth surface of his lower jaw, the feathery lines at the corners of his eyes. And she knew what night he was talking about, too.

"Why bring that up?" she asked quietly, turning away again.

She looked beautiful, soft and clean and womanly, and he kept looking at her. "It happened, Katie. Pretending it didn't won't change it."

Her skin prickled at his tone, his familiarity. "I wish you wouldn't call me Katie."

"Don't change the subject. Talk to me about it. Haven't you ever wondered why that night happened? I was older, but I really have only a faint memory of the valley before you came along."

Kate spoke with very little emotion. "My mother brought me here and left me with Granddad when I was four."

"Why? Where did she go?"

"My dad was dead, so Granddad told me. She…just couldn't take care of me, I guess. Anyway, she came back a few times, and when I was seven, we got word that she'd died, too. A car accident. There are details, some of them not very pretty."

Cooper's eyes reflected more emotion than Kate's voice. "Orphans, both of us. Thank God we had Sam and Les, Kate."

"Yes."

He took her detachment as controlled distress. "You're bitter about it, aren't you?"

"Not bitter. I've long accepted it, and it's not a subject I get all worked up about anymore."

"That night, Katie, we'd been friends for so many years, and…"

Kate sat up abruptly. "I don't want to discuss it, Cooper. There's nothing to discuss, anyway. If you're looking for a reason, just lay it on foolishness, for both of us."

Scooting up, Cooper leaned his back against the tree trunk again. "You'd never been with a man before."

She laughed sharply. "Of course not. I'd never even had a normal date." Her eyes found him briefly, cynically. "Maybe I was just curious."

"About me, or men in general?"

"Oh, please! Is this why you suggested a ride together, so you could quiz me?"

"No, but I got thinking about it on the way up here. I'll tell you something, Kate. I don't believe you've never wondered why we came together like we did. You're an intelligent, bright woman, but even a dull-witted one would remember the first man she'd made love with and maybe wonder why she'd chosen him."

"Chosen?" Kate gave him a disbelieving look. "Surely you don't think I deliberately chose what happened! I don't remember it as a matter of choice. It just…just happened!" Too agitated to sit there any longer, Kate started to get up. But before she got very far, Cooper moved quickly, took her by the arms and brought her across his lap. Startled, she stared into his eyes.

"Just be still," he said in a strange, hoarse voice. "Nothing's going to happen that you don't want."

His knees were at her back, supporting her, and his hands held her upper arms. Her heart had started thumping, and she wondered if she wasn't going to do something stupid, like let the hot tears behind her eyes spill out. Her emotions were raw where Cooper was concerned, especially since those almost insane thoughts of being in love with him had staggered her.

His eyes were dark and intense. "I told you last night I was drawn to you. It's an old feeling, Kate, one that's been banked for ten years. If you hadn't come back, maybe it would have stayed banked." He studied her. "Say something."

Her tongue flicked, dampening her lips. "Say what?" she whispered, then cleared her throat and found her voice. "I thought all you wanted was friendship. Friends don't haul each other on their laps, Cooper."

His smile was rather grim. "You're a sexy woman. Maybe we can't be only friends." He shook his head then, as if surprised by this turn and trying to deal with it. "I didn't plan to make a pass."

Kate felt his gaze on her mouth, and she knew she should do everything in her power to prevent a kiss. That's what he was thinking about; she could see it in his eyes. But this was Cooper, and she could call herself names, disloyal, traitorous, stupid, and more, and still want his kiss. His eyes contained a richness, a depth of feeling, and she knew it could only be desire because she felt the same thing developing where her backside connected with the front of his jeans.

He was getting aroused just from this, although holding her in this fashion was certainly intimate enough. Her arousal wasn't quite so apparent, although Kate certainly knew that her nipples were puckered and aching, and the throb between her legs too intense to ignore.

"Maybe you wouldn't object if I kissed you," he said softly.

"Maybe…I wouldn't," she whispered.

His face came down slowly, almost cautiously, and his lips barely touched hers. Then he looked at her questioningly. "Would you have objected that night in Reno?"

She thought, then nodded. "Yes, I think I would have."

"I thought so." His mouth brushed hers again, and then he let her arms go to cup her face. His hands felt big and warm, and comforting in a way that stunned Kate. "I see so much when I look at you, Kate. Years, literally, time and things I'd almost forgotten. I see you as you were and as you are now."

A rush of blood seemed to be racing wildly through her body. "I see you that way, too. At moments you're younger and the Cooper I remember, and at other times.…" She was speaking too freely, too honestly, and she stopped herself.

"Kate, there are so many memories between us."

"You…weren't always kind," she whispered.

"I wasn't?" She saw that he was genuinely surprised, and again realized that even their shared memories contained personal slants. This was so very, very dangerous, and Kate searched her heart and soul for the strength to break away. Most of the past was irrevocable, and if she started seeing it through Cooper's eyes…?

Those beautiful blue eyes, looking down at her with

so much warmth. Her heart skittered as they came closer. He had a wonderful mouth, and she felt it circling her own. Then the wet slickness of the tip of his tongue. Her eyes closed.

The pressure of his lips on hers increased gradually, along with the wild beating of her heart, the rhythmic pulsing of her blood. His hands threaded into her hair, and she could feel the strength of his fingers, each one, on her scalp. His knees came up higher, raising her, bringing her closer, until her breasts pushed against his chest.

Kate had a sense of reunion, of rediscovery, when they had never kissed each other enough for her to feel so at home in his arms. That one night was all there'd been between them, and one night so long ago shouldn't be enough that every cell in her body remembered.

Her hands crept up his shoulders, to the back of his neck, to the springy, bristly hair there. His tongue moved into her mouth, slipping past her parted lips, and her body responded with throbs and tingles. He nibbled her lower lip, and they both caught much needed breaths. "Kate..." A ragged edge was on the word, a wealth of wanting that dizzied her even more than she already was.

Love beat in Kate's breast, and she was beyond refusing it. She could wish she didn't care so much, but she couldn't stop it, or turn it around, not even when some of the bad memories intruded. "Oh, Cooper," she huskily whispered.

"Katie, you're sweet and so beautiful."

Their mouths mated again, a union of increasing desire. His hips lifted, thrusting his maleness against her, and a big hand found enough space between them to cover a breast. A wild thrill rocketed through Kate's body, reaching even her limbs, culminating in a spiraling heat in her loins. His palm chafed her nipple through her shirt, and she was glad she hadn't worn a bra. Her breasts were small and firm, and she often went without a bra, having begun her adulthood despising being bound up, an old preference that still influenced her way of dressing.

Kate felt her reserve melting away, layer after layer of the old resentments flicking away. His lips teased and tasted and commanded, and he relaxed the bend of his knees, giving him access to the buttons on her shirt. His head came up, his mouth leaving her kiss-wet lips, and their gazes locked while he slowly worked the buttons through their tiny openings. Kate searched his eyes, wanting to see just a hint of what she was feeling, of the love she now knew reached back through time and trials, casting old hurts aside in its wake as if they were of small import. She saw heat, and the glaze of desire, and she didn't know if there was more. She wondered then what he could see in her eyes. Or if he cared enough to look beyond the obvious.

He gently pushed the panels of her opened shirt apart, and she felt the breath he sucked in at the sight of her bare breasts. Physically, he was strongly affected by her; emotionally, Kate just didn't know. His fingers were tender on her nipples, and shafts of shooting pleasure traveled that mysterious pathway between breasts and the core of her femaleness.

She wanted him; she'd always wanted him. He was the handsome hero of her youth, her first love. In all honesty, her only love.

But Kate knew, as surely as she knew where this

was leading, that Cooper didn't see *her* as a heroine. She'd disrupted his life and threatened his peace, and if she remembered anything about the Sinclairs, both Cooper and Sam, it was that they'd been fighters. Digging just a little deeper into that thought, Kate had to wonder just what method of battle Cooper was using in her case.

And then it hit her. He'd put off even thinking about the lawsuit until Labor Day? My God, how could she have been so naive as to even consider believing him? He'd put nothing off! It had flashed through her mind briefly that night in Reno, that he was using delaying tactics with the hope she would change her mind about suing him. But she hadn't thought he would stoop so low as to make love to her to influence her decision!

Quite deliberately Kate took his hands away from her breasts. "That's enough," she said coldly.

Startled bewilderment widened his eyes. "What's the matter?"

Kate slid off his lap and got to her feet. With her back to him she quickly buttoned her shirt and tucked its loosened tails into the waist of her jeans. Showing him her back wasn't because of a sudden burst of maidenly modesty; she needed a minute to blink back the hot, angry tears stinging her eyes.

"Kate?" Cooper stood up. "What's wrong?"

"Nothing."

"Damn it, don't get female on me! Your lips are swollen from kisses you wanted as much as I did. You kissed me back, Kate. Then you just stopped. Something went through that head of yours. What was it?"

She wanted to tell him. She wanted to turn and shriek at him, to cuss him out as she'd done as a teenager. But she wasn't a teenager now, and she'd already handled the summer badly enough. She started for Shadow.

Cooper lunged forward and caught her by the arm. "Kate, this is silly. Talk to me."

She glanced down and saw the strained fabric of his fly. He was excited, worked up and frustrated because she'd said no. Her eyes leveled on his face. "It's not going to happen again, Cooper. I'm not eighteen and naive now." *Oh, yeah?* Wincing at just how easily Cooper had manipulated her since her arrival, Kate shrugged his hand away and picked up Shadow's reins.

"We've both grown up, Kate, not just you. Can't you recognize honest feelings when you see them? Damn it, when you *feel* them?"

She looked at him, hard. "You're so transparent, Cooper, you make me sick!"

"*What?*" Stunned, Cooper backed up three paces. But astonishment rolled away quickly, and in its place a black, defensive anger narrowed his eyes. "Do you even know what the hell you're talking about? What do you mean, I'm transparent?"

Kate's green eyes blazed. "Cooper, I'm not going to get into a big hassle over this."

"You're not. Well, that's just great. Just what makes you think you can start something like this and then walk away?"

"*Me* start something? Come off it, Cooper. You're only ticked off because I said no. Your ego got just a little bit bruised. Apparently you're not accustomed to women saying no." Kate recoiled when he barked out a harsh four-letter word, and she was relieved when he spun around and walked off. Quickly she swung up into the saddle. "I'm starting back," she said to the angry contours of his back.

Without a word Cooper walked over to Monty and mounted the big horse. The little procession stayed intact until it reached the valley floor, with neither Cooper nor Kate so much as glancing at the other.

Then, without warning, Cooper turned his horse's head away from the most direct way back. "I'm sure you can find your way home alone," he said coldly.

Kate's chin came up. "I'm sure I can."

Two days later Kate saw the helicopter leaving the valley. It was early morning, and the blue and white bird's raucous rotors shattered the quiet until it disappeared through the river's canyon.

Kate left the kitchen window and resumed the chair she'd been using at the table before she'd heard the copter. She picked up her coffee mug, put her elbows on the table and held the mug with both hands, sipping from it thoughtfully. How long would it be before Cooper came back for another few days?

Despite the undoubtable anger they'd parted with, it had surprised Kate that Cooper had stayed away. She was positive she understood his game plan now, or she had been positive by the time she'd ridden Shadow all the way back home that afternoon. Get Kate in the sack, get her so sexually involved she would never dream of suing her lover. The more she'd thought about it, the more sense it had made. From Cooper's viewpoint, of course.

Her viewpoint was clouded and badly dented. She'd accused Cooper of reacting to a bruised ego, but Kate wondered if hers hadn't been permanently destroyed. She couldn't think of Cooper and love in the same

breath, but she knew that a part of herself belonged to
him and always would.

The lure of Mustang Valley had gradually dissi-
pated. It was lonely, and, without family, just plain
forlorn. The old house, even with all the painting and
cleaning she'd done, *was* practically falling down, and
besides, she'd run out of things she could do to im-
prove it without money. The nostalgia of memory it
invoked was something to put aside, to leave in the
past.

Picturing the long weeks of summer ahead, Kate
saw herself as aimless and living for Cooper's occasional visits. The bottom line of the whole episode
was, she was ready to wash her hands of the valley,
the water rights, and yes, of Cooper.

She'd thought she'd had such powerful ammunition
before she got here. But there was no way Katherine
Redmond was ever going to bring Cooper Sinclair to
his knees. Even if he finally agreed to sign over the
original Redmond land to her, he would tie it up some
way. Even in New York Kate had anticipated Cooper
demanding a buy-sell agreement should he lose the
battle. It wouldn't be at all out of the ordinary, either.
If she ever wanted to sell, she would have to give
Cooper first right of refusal.

It all boiled down to money in the end, and Kate
knew now that she couldn't make her home in the
valley. Cooper had seen to that.

Well, maybe it wasn't quite fair to put the entire
blame for such a change of heart on him. It really
wasn't his fault that she hadn't found what she'd
hoped for here. It simply wasn't possible to go back,
not when most of the players were missing. Sam dead,
Les dead, Cooper living in Reno most of the time.

Kate put the mug down and covered her face with her hands. She rubbed her eyes with her fingertips, a weary, defeated gesture. It was time to close the chapter on this fiasco and get on with her life. And she knew exactly what she had to do to prevent any future ideas from tempting her into returning to Mustang Valley, too. She was certain Cooper would be only too glad to go along with it.

Seven

Cooper paced the small balcony overlooking the casino, three steps one way, three back.

Ever since he'd returned to Reno from the ranch, he'd cursed his stupidity with Kate. He'd vowed to expand their friendship and had instead behaved like a sex-starved adolescent. Why hadn't he kept his hands to himself, and why, for God's sake, had he gotten so ridiculously angry when she'd put a stop to things?

The din from the first floor grated on Cooper's nerves. He didn't want to be in the midst of crowds and noise; he wanted to be in the valley. He wanted to see Kate. What was she doing today? Why had he let stubborn pride stop him from going to see her again before he left Mustang Valley? He'd been in Reno for three days and had been having a hell of a time getting any work done.

If he could even call Kate. No telephone in that old house was a pain in the neck and frustrating. She seemed so out of reach, as if she were a thousand miles away.

Cooper walked back into his office, closed the door and plopped into the chair behind his desk. After scowling at the telephone for a minute, he picked it up and dialed his ranch number. "Leila, this is Cooper. Is Dirk close at hand, by any chance?"

"I'm sure I can locate him, Coop, but he's not in the house."

"Would you do that, please, and have him call me as soon as possible?"

"Certainly."

With a brief "Thanks, Leila," Cooper put the phone down. Then he sat back, ignoring the stacks of letters and other work demanding attention on his desk. A deep, abiding anger was like a fist in his belly.

Why in hell was he here when he didn't want to be? He had more money than he could possibly spend in three lifetimes, and even with the many fine charities he regularly donated large sums to, his bank account just kept growing. He didn't need any more money, he didn't *want* any more money.

What he wanted was Mustang Valley. Thinking of the peace of the valley versus what was going on in this building made Cooper feel ill. A thought struck him with the impact of a battering ram: if he never saw a casino or hotel again, he would never miss either.

His intercom rang, and he pressed a button. "Dirk is on line three," his secretary told him.

"Thanks, Kathy." Cooper picked up the telephone. "Dirk? I need a favor."

"Anything, Coop. What is it?"

"Go over to Kate Redmond's place and ask her to give me a call. She can use a phone at the ranch. Tell her it's important."

After Dirk had agreed and hung up, Cooper dialed David Walker's number. It was a minute before the attorney came on the line, but then Cooper got right to the point. "I've decided to sell Sinclair's, Dave. Before I start spreading the word around, would you set up an appointment to meet with my accountants? I want to be sure all of my records are up-to-date and in first-class shape. The place will sell fast, and I don't want any legal hitches halfway through a deal."

The attorney was stunned, Cooper could tell. Sinclair's was a plum, and once the word hit the street, buyers would be lined up for a crack at it.

Cooper had one more call to make, an interoffice communiqué. Jack Leonard, his able assistant, deserved to hear about his plans before anyone else in the organization. "I'd like us to have lunch together, Jack. There's something I have to go over with you."

With the wheels well in motion, Cooper settled down to work. He felt much better, elated even. Getting started on something that had been gradually gaining prominence in the back of his mind for years was like losing a hundred pound burden.

Kate was his only loose end now, her and her lawsuit. The possible court action didn't bother Cooper nearly as much as Kate, herself, though. She had reentered his life like a small tornado, stirring up long-forgotten memories, trying his patience and raising his libido. One night beside a river ten years ago should not seem like the sexual highlight of his life, but it did. Adding to his confusion, Cooper kept getting glimpses of something deeper and more lasting than a desire for mere physical gratification when he thought of Kate. She was an intriguing woman and causing him more discomfort than he liked.

The intercom buzzed again. "A Katherine Redmond is on line two, Cooper," Kathy announced.

"Thanks." Cooper punched the button and grabbed up the receiver. "Kate?"

"Yes. Dirk said you needed to speak to me."

Her husky voice was like a melody in his ear, urging a smile, and a wonderful relief because she didn't sound angry relaxed Cooper's tension. He spoke with warmth, "Thanks for calling right away."

"You're welcome. Actually, I need to talk to you, too." Kate was sitting in Cooper's own den at his ranch. She had been planning to call him, anyway, and Dirk's message had only prodded her to action a little sooner than she might have done on her own.

Cooper wasn't at all prepared to hear, "I'm going back to New York, but I need to see you before I leave. Do you have any idea when you'll be back in the valley?"

Every vestige of Cooper's smile disappeared. "Going? For how long?"

"For good. I shouldn't have come to Nevada in the first place."

Momentarily speechless, Cooper finally managed a hoarse, "I don't understand, Kate. If you're leaving because of what happened at Coyote Creek..."

"I'd rather not get into that, if you don't mind," Kate interrupted. "My decision..."

"But that's why I had to talk to you! Kate, I'm sorry for behaving like a schoolboy. My God, don't leave the valley because of..."

"My decision is final, Cooper. I really must see you before I go, however. When will you be home again?"

Cooper couldn't think clearly. Kate, leaving? Why? What about the lawsuit? What the hell was going through her mind now? "I just don't get it," he mumbled into the phone.

"You will."

"Can't you tell me what this is all about right now?"

"I'd rather not."

He tried to interpret the nuances of her voice. Maybe she *was* angry. What, really, was he hearing? She sounded distant, but other than that, he couldn't read her mood. He thought about his decision to sell Sinclair's, about his lunch date with Jack, about the overwhelming myriad of details to take care of here to activate that decision.

But whatever was going on with Kate had to be dealt with, too, and somehow he must find the time. "I'll get there as soon as I can," he said with a brusqueness born out of suddenly realizing just how much he did have to do. Selling Sinclair's would be a time-consuming process.

One didn't transfer ownership of this kind of property like one did a house. The Nevada Gaming Commission watched gaming properties with an eagle eye, making sure that no one involved in any sort of criminal activities profited from gambling revenues. Undesirables were not welcome in Nevada, and the Gaming Commission's stamp of approval was necessary before a casino could change hands.

Kate wasn't satisfied with Cooper's vague answer. He was a busy man, yes, but her time meant something, too, if only to herself. The document she had drawn up in the last few days weighted her mind. She wanted this final confrontation over and done with. "In the next few days?" she insisted.

"Yes, in the next few days."

"I'll see you then." Kate quietly put the phone down and got up from behind the desk. After talking to Leila for a few minutes, she left Cooper's house and drove back to her own.

That afternoon Kate took Shadow out for a long ride. The nostalgia of the valley brought tears to her eyes several different times. It was such a beautiful place, she thought with profound sadness. The mountains ringing the valley seemed like a picture frame, or a protective fence line, isolating its green fields, winding river and scattered groves of trees from the rest of the world.

Mustang Valley retained a sense of untouched timelessness. Only northern Nevada's changing seasons influenced the beauty of the valley, as little beyond nature had the power to infiltrate the mountains' barrier.

Cooper belonged here, Kate thought with a deep pang. Just as Les Redmond and Sam Sinclair had belonged here. It hurt terribly to admit again, and to see with almost blinding clarity, that she was an outsider now, an intruder. Not that she longed for New York. What she longed for was the past, those impossible to recapture rosy days of her youth. That, more than anything else, was what had brought her back. Too bad she hadn't seen that before she came, Kate thought on a long sigh.

Turning Shadow's head, Kate began to follow the river's path. As she knew she would, she came to the bend where she and Cooper had made love so long ago. Sliding from the saddle, Kate looped the reins over a low bush. Then she walked over to the riverbank, found the exact spot where she'd been sitting that night, and sank down on the large rock.

Staring at the moving water, Kate wiped at another tear. Her emotions were raw and close to the surface. Leaving the valley and Cooper was the only sensible course, but she'd gotten no pleasure out of telling him about it on the phone. He'd seemed rather stunned, but that was probably to be expected when she'd been so adamant about spending the summer here only a short time ago. In the end, though, when she gave him that document, he would be extremely relieved.

Kate thought about the document. The day after Cooper had left for Reno, she had drawn up a conveyance of water rights. It was written by hand, but she had located a notary public and had her signature notarized. When Cooper ultimately filed the conveyance with the county recorder's office, he would legally own all of Mustang Valley's water rights. Kate intended asking only one thing in return, that he buy her hundred acres from her.

It was to be a final, irrevocable break with Mustang Valley, with Nevada and with Cooper. She would never come back here again.

The helicopter's noise barely penetrated Cooper's brooding thoughts. *Why are you leaving, Katie? What about your lawsuit? What about the water rights? Damn it, what about me?*

The questions had hounded him all through lunch with Jack while he'd explained his plans to sell Sinclair's. Jack had been understandably upset. A lot of people were going to be upset, Cooper knew. He had many faithful, loyal employees, and that aspect of the sale was disturbing. He'd assured Jack and promised himself that he would impress upon Sinclair's future owner how invaluable Jack and some of the other longtime employees were to the business.

In the air now and on his way to Mustang Valley, however, Cooper's thoughts were on Kate, not on the multitude of problems he'd put on hold in Reno. Why would she leave now when she'd planned to stay the summer? Unless...

Good Lord. Had he botched things so badly that she'd changed her mind about waiting until fall to file her suit? Was that why she had to see him before she left, to tell him she would be handling the case from New York?

The thought of a long-distance legal battle made Cooper wince. On the other hand, the thought of Kate leaving at all made his stomach churn. He really didn't want Kate to go, and the feeling had nothing to do with water rights or lawsuits, either. It had to do with Kate herself, with the sunny-honey color of her hair, and the way her mouth turned up at its corners. It had to do with how she sat a horse, and the cool green of her eyes.

It had to do with how she felt in his arms.

Lord above, was he falling for Kate?

Twilight was threatening when the helicopter approached the valley. The view was silvery and peaceful, but there was nothing peaceful about the turmoil in Cooper's gut.

Kate stepped out of the shower, wrapped a towel around her wet hair and dried off with another. After folding and returning the bath towel to its rack, Kate slipped into a bright pink terry robe. On the way to her bedroom, she unwound the towel from around her head and used it to briskly rub moisture from her hair.

It wasn't late, but it was getting dark, and she snapped on the lamp on the dresser. The file folder containing her papers drew her notice, and she opened it and scanned the topmost document reflectively. She was all ready for that final meeting with Cooper, if and when he deigned to show up.

Sighing, Kate walked about the bedroom while she towel-dried her hair. The months since she'd discovered the water rights error lingered in her mind. She'd handled the whole thing badly. Not because she was an inadequate attorney, but if she ever performed that ineptly for a client, she would never forgive herself. Kate knew very well if a client had come to her with the documents and case she had, she would have advised a much different course than the one she had followed.

Her mistake had been in confronting Cooper. She had allowed a personal desire to see a Sinclair squirm ruin her own case. Oh, not that she couldn't still file the suit. But doing so before Labor Day would be unethical, and the sad truth was, the whole thing had lost impetus. Besides, not only hadn't Cooper squirmed, he hadn't even wiggled. For the sake of her own mental health, the sooner she left Mustang Valley and put Cooper back in the past, the better off she'd be.

As for that strange, piercing ache that kept shifting homes in her body, it would eventually abate. She had survived without Cooper for ten years, and she would manage to do so again.

On edge over the entire matter, Kate switched on

the small bedside radio, hoping some music would help her nerves. Fiddling with the dial, she finally located a reasonably clear station playing country music. With the silence of the evening banished, Kate went to the mirror above the dresser. Her hair was thick and dried slowly, unless she used her electric dryer, and it hung in damp curls around her face.

Kate tensed then, striving to identify the sound she had just heard. A car? She went to the window and peered out, catching a glimpse of someone going around the corner of the house, apparently seeking the back door.

Dashing through the house to the kitchen, Kate switched on the ceiling light. The visitor knocked on the door. "I'm coming," she called, then at the door, "Who is it?"

"Cooper."

Cooper! Kate took a hasty assessment of her appearance and rated it a big fat zero. She couldn't have looked worse had she tried!

Resentful that he would catch her looking like this, Kate yanked the door open. "You could have told me you were coming tonight!"

She looked about seventeen with her shiny-clean face and pink robe, even with her eyes flashing angry sparks. "I decided I better get here and find out what's going on. May I come in?"

Kate's exasperation showed. This wasn't at all how she'd planned their final meeting. But then, had any of her plans worked out? "Yes, you may come in. But you'll have to entertain yourself while I get dressed."

Cooper's gaze traveled down to the bare toes peeking from the bottom of her robe, then back up. "You don't have to get dressed for my sake. You look great.''

Oh, sure. Tell me another one! ''I'll only be a few minutes. There's lemonade and cold beer in the refrigerator. Help yourself.''

Kate was gone in a flash. In the bedroom she grabbed a sundress with a splashy print fabric out of the closet, got rid of the robe and pulled the dress on without slowing down for underwear.

At the mirror she grimaced at her hair and admitted there was nothing she could do with it that wouldn't take at least fifteen minutes. She quickly dusted a bit of blusher on her cheeks, applied a touch of lip gloss, took a deep breath and started out of the bedroom. Remembering her bare feet at the last second, she hurried back to the closet for a pair of sandals.

Kate stopped then, needing a minute to calm herself. Her heart was pounding like a frightened deer's, which was too adolescent for words. Adding to her general discomfort, the house felt hot and stuffy, as it always did at the end of a warm day. Kate closed her eyes, reaching for composure. Being the instigator of this meeting was reason enough for anxiety, but a girlish breathlessness was ridiculous. Enough was enough. Cooper was only a man.

Oh, if that were only true!

In five minutes flat, breathing only slightly easier, Kate walked into the kitchen. Cooper was holding a beer and leaning against the sink counter. He blinked twice. ''That has to be some kind of record.''

Ignoring the comment, Kate opened the refrigerator door and took out the pitcher of lemonade. ''It wasn't necessary that you come right away. I hope I didn't give you that impression on the phone today.''

"What you gave me on the phone upset the hell out of me."

Amazed, Kate turned to face him. Yes, he looked upset, if thinly pursed lips and a dark glower were any measure. "Why?" she questioned flatly. If Cooper had arrived with a chip on his shoulder, he just might find out she wasn't in the greatest of moods herself.

"Why *wouldn't* I be upset? This is rather sudden, isn't it? What happened to spending the summer here?"

Frowning, Kate finished pouring lemonade into a glass, then returned the pitcher to the refrigerator. She wouldn't understand Cooper Sinclair if she lived to be a hundred. One would think he'd be turning handsprings over seeing the last of her. At least, once she handed over that document, she could quit trying to unravel what went on behind those blue eyes. "Let's sit in the living room."

They carried their drinks to the next room and sat down. Cooper looked around. The furniture was old and the wallpaper faded, but the woodwork had been painted and everything was spotlessly clean. "You've worked hard here."

"I don't like dirt." Kate took a swallow of lemonade. She didn't want to stare, but Cooper looked incredible, wearing pale gray slacks, a black shirt and black loafers, obviously clothing from his Reno Wardrobe. He'd come so soon, and she hadn't expected him to drop everything and rush to see her. She also hadn't expected him to begin this meeting with an admission—which had sounded an awful lot like an accusation, now that she thought about it—of being upset because she was leaving. The man was a damned enigma, a mass of contradictions.

Cooper was staring, too, but, unlike Kate, wasn't trying to hide it. He loved her dress. It had been a dozen different colors, blues, aquas, pinks and greens, a tropical pattern that was stunning with her tan. Her hair had no particular style, just half-dried curls springing every which way, and he remembered how straight her hair used to be. It was obviously permed now and only reached her shoulders, but the color was the same glorious rainbow of sun-kissed tones.

Still staring, Cooper bluntly asked, "Why are you leaving?"

Kate had no intention of answering that question precisely. That would involve him and feelings she didn't dare confess. Upset or not, he would hear only what she wanted him to hear. "Personal reasons," she said evenly.

"Oh." Cooper frowned with a brand new thought. It hadn't even occurred to him before this that Kate might have left someone important behind in New York. It should have, he realized. Kate was too exciting, too interesting, to be without an admirer. "I suppose you're talking about a man," he said slowly.

Surprise stopped Kate cold. A second surprise was a realization that she didn't want Cooper thinking she had a man waiting in New York. Or anywhere else, for that matter.

"I'm not leaving because of a man," was a good effort, but sounded pretty sappy when she instantly saw the fallacy in the positive statement. She almost laughed, although not out of humor. There wasn't anything very funny in Cooper being the cause of her early departure, than supposing she was rushing back to New York because of a man. It was ironic, not funny.

Cooper's frankly skeptical stare was perturbing. "Then, why?" he persisted.

Kate fidgeted. The document in the bedroom was gnawing at her, but picturing herself going to get it and slapping it into Cooper's hand was demoralizing. Which was silly. She'd prepared to give it to him, so why was she hesitating now? This meeting could be over in five minutes, if she could just persuade herself to get out of this chair and go get that document.

Kate registered Cooper's abnormally stern expression. He looked tired, too, and impatient. She watched him finish his beer, then crumple the can, a gesture of aggravation. "Would you like another?" she asked.

"No. What I'd like is some straight talk. Damn it, Kate, I left a pile of work to get here, and…"

"Which was completely unnecessary. I never asked you to drop everything, did I?"

"Not in so many words, no. But you knocked me for a loop on the phone. I've wondered all day why you decided to leave so suddenly. You must have a reason. Why are you being so damned evasive?"

Her gaze settled on him, then darted away. Seeing Cooper again, being in the same room with him, was blurring Kate's previous resolve. Disturbing, too, was the knowledge that giving him that document would eliminate any need whatsoever for further communication between them. Why had that seemed so sensible before and now seemed only sad? Such ambivalence was extremely destructive, Kate knew, and unlike her.

He was determined to get some kind of answer from her, Kate saw, and squared her shoulders in preparation of a bout of *real* evasiveness. "It's just that I don't see any good reason to hang around here all summer."

Cooper cocked an eyebrow. "Are you saying you'll be back after Labor Day in that case?"

"No...well...I'm not sure."

Pinning her with a hard look did nothing but make her squirm a little. "You're hedging, Kate. Maybe you're even lying."

Kate bristled. "That's rather rude, don't you think?"

Cooper stared. He was getting nowhere, and the urge to shake this frustrating, maddening woman was getting stronger by the minute. He got up, only because he couldn't sit there any longer. "Fine! So I'm rude. Let's try this from another angle. You said you had to see me before you left. You shouldn't have any trouble explaining what *that* was all about."

Kate bit her lip. "Yes, I did, didn't I?" She felt so foolish. Cooper was furious, and could she really blame him? All she had to do was go into the bedroom, get the document and hand it over. It would explain everything. But her decision to leave seemed so hasty now. And she wished she knew why her options kept changing priority. Or, why, all of a sudden, she even *had* any options. Until Cooper showed up, everything was so clear. Not wonderful, but certainly clear.

Actually, she knew why, Kate thought uncomfortably. When Cooper was around, she was a different woman. He affected her in alarming ways. Her most female side reacted to him without direction or intention from her brain. Looking way, way back, Kate could see that nothing had changed in that respect. Cooper had always affected her, provoking strong emotions. That was why she'd either loved or hated him as a girl.

What bothered her even more, though, was how muddled her thinking was around him now. Alone, as she'd been so much of the time since her arrival to the valley, she was able to sort things out, to make sensible decisions and to act upon those decisions. In his presence, nothing was clear-cut or even seemed particularly rational.

Right at the moment Kate was hard-pressed to label her feelings for Cooper as love, as she had during their horseback ride to Coyote Creek. In retrospect, that had been a strange moment, as if years of emotional cloud layers had suddenly parted and a shattering but extremely distinct truth had dropped on her.

One of the problems with that memory was what had come after; Cooper trying to make love to her. That was another point that seemed so fuzzy to Kate now. Had he really hoped to influence her determination about that lawsuit with a sexual involvement?

Kate recognized how discouraged and disenchanted she was with the whole thing now. It was best to give Cooper that document and be done with this fiasco once and for all. He was spitting mad, and maybe she was, too. If for no other reason than because he was Sam Sinclair's grandson!

She got up. Cooper's eyes narrowed. "Kate, what's going on? First, you won't tell me why you're leaving, and now you won't talk about whatever it is you referred to on the phone. You said specifically that you needed to talk to me, and that I would understand everything when I got here. Well, I'm here, and I still don't know a damned thing!"

"Don't raise your voice to me," Kate returned sharply.

Exasperated, Cooper ran his fingers through his hair.

"Do you have any idea what I left behind to get here? No, you couldn't."

He really did seem unusually keyed up, Kate admitted to herself. Maybe something was amiss in Reno, and if he'd hurried to the valley because of her remarks on the phone, she was sorry. But nothing was explicit or well defined between the two of them, neither actions nor emotions, and they didn't communicate very well. Starting with personal slants on their respective grandfathers, and proceeding to the valley, the water rights and every moment they'd ever shared, they were really as far apart as two people could be. It was a sad summation of their relationship, but only a fool would disregard it.

Kate took a few steps toward the door, fully intending on finally getting that document and placing it in Cooper's hands. She had procrastinated long enough.

"Where are you going?"

"I'll only be a minute."

"Damn it, Kate!"

Why, he really was furious! Startled, Kate stopped to give him a searching look. "What are you so angry about?"

Cooper didn't deny the accusation. He *was* angry. He was tired and impatient and more upset than he'd been in ages. Kate calmly announcing plans to leave and then acting as though it should mean nothing to him was a kick he couldn't seem to handle. And dropping everything the way he had to get here and then getting nothing from Kate in explanation was irking as hell. "About your dissemination, for one thing. Why won't you give me a straight answer?"

Kate's eyes were blazing. "I plan to, but don't try to push your damned Sinclair weight around here! I don't have to scrape and bow to you just because you're in some kind of weird, demanding mood.''

''My mood is because of you!''

''And don't yell at me! Just who do you think you are? I could have gone back to New York without ever seeing you again, but I delayed my own plans to...''

When Kate's voice just stopped, Cooper scowled. ''To what? Are you purposely trying to drive me crazy?''

Kate turned away. ''Oh, stop being ridiculous,'' she muttered, and started for the door again. Before she reached it, she felt big hands grab her shoulders and spin her around. Kate's own fury erupted then, but when she saw Cooper's face, the gush of angry words in her throat choked down to a lump.

The next thing she knew, she was being yanked forward into a rough embrace.

Eight

Kate's head began spinning. She hadn't expected a pass, not with so much opposition in the air. Cooper's arms were pinning hers to her sides, and there was nothing tender on his face. He looked tense and impatient, she realized, revising her first impulsive thoughts about a pass. As usual, she didn't know what was going on in Cooper's mind. Staring up at him with a sprouting uncertainty, she demanded, in a show of bravado, "What's *this* all about?"

His eyes were midnight-dark and hard. "You're driving me up the wall. Do you know that?"

"That's silly! What have I done to drive you up the wall?"

"Talk in riddles and evade direct answers, for starters. Just what the hell's going on, Kate?" Cooper's hands moved to her shoulders, and he gave her a slight shake, as one might do to subjugate a petulant child.

A crimson stain marked Kate's cheeks. If there was one thing that could stir up old indignities, it was Cooper acting like a damned Sinclair! "You're as overbearing as you always were. Take your hands off me!"

He didn't obey. His eyes held hers in a stare-down that lasted until Kate finally exploded. "I said...!"

"I know what you said. Katie..."

His voice had softened, his eyes, too. And suddenly Kate's knees were weak and mushy. So quickly, *too* quickly, he was able to remind her of the past and to raise emotions better left alone. "Don't, Cooper," she whispered.

His hands moved on her shoulders, a sliding caress that magnified the sudden chemistry between them. Kate felt her own feelings tumbling one on top of the other, such forceful feelings, love, resentment, even some hatred. Years of feelings were in this room with them, years of memories, a thousand small details that danced and darted through Kate's mind.

Underlying them all was her plan to leave. If everything worked out, this would be the very last time she would be with Cooper. Kate felt herself wilting, with the dissension and bitterness of the distant past and even the last few minutes losing distinction.

The bare skin of her shoulders felt like warm satin to Cooper's hands. She was so pretty, but the beauty of Kate's face was secondary to her aura of sensuality. She had radiated that same disturbing quality years ago, but when he'd noticed it then, she'd been too young. He'd kept her in the kid sister category until that night by the river, and then age hadn't mattered, not hers, not his.

She wasn't too young now, and standing so close

to her and touching her like this, Cooper knew he'd wanted her from the moment he'd walked into his study and seen her that first day.

"Katie," he murmured again, and slowly lowered his face. It didn't surprise him that she didn't back away or make some kind of protest. He felt her changing mood right through her skin and saw it on her face. Whatever was going on with Kate, she wasn't going to stop him from kissing her.

He didn't question it. His mouth covered hers and found it soft and pliant. His pulse rate increased until he could hear his own heartbeat in his ears. His arms tightened around her, drawing her closer, and became tighter still when he felt her leaning into him. Somehow her arms were around his neck, and then they were straining together.

Her response was dizzying. It was natural and real and emotional, exactly as it had been that night by the river. For the very first time Cooper was able to really understand what happened that night. What man could resist a woman who gave so freely?

Their mouths caressed as kiss melted into kiss. Kate felt so right in his arms, and Cooper had never been bashful. His tongue slipped between her lips while his hands began moving on her back. The dress stopped just below her shoulder blades. He explored its straps, but kept returning to the bare skin between them.

A moment for breathing allowed Kate to speak. The turmoil in her blood made her voice low and husky. "Why are you doing this?"

Cooper looked deeply into her eyes. "We, Kate, we."

"All right, I'm willing to share the responsibility. Why are we doing this?"

"Do we really need a reason?" He stroked the springy curls around her face with a tenderness that nearly undid Kate. Cooper had the power to surprise her in so many ways. She'd told herself repeatedly that he only wanted to ensnare her into a sexual relationship because of her potential lawsuit, but that theory was beginning to lose appeal. Maybe she only *wanted* it to lose appeal, she was still rational enough to speculate. Standing against Cooper with his arms around her was terribly influencing. He was big and warm and sexy and...Cooper.

And, God help her, she did love him. She resented his name, she resented what the Sinclairs had done to the Redmonds, she resented Cooper's secure, lifetime possession of the valley. But she was deeply, eternally in love with him.

Kate felt the last remnants of fight draining from her system. The water rights document in the bedroom could disintegrate right now for all she cared. She was in Cooper's arms. He'd rushed to the valley because he'd been upset about her plans to leave, and that surely meant something, didn't it?

It was a strange moment. They had kissed one another with undoubtable passion, and then Cooper had become tender. The passion was still in his eyes, though, and they were standing close enough together for Kate to know how physically aroused he was.

She made up her mind and moved closer still. Cooper's eyes narrowed, but he didn't hesitate to heed the invitation. His mouth opened on hers with a muffled groan. This kiss was hungry, devouring, and lasted until their lungs were bursting. "Kate...Katie," he whispered thickly, catching her bottom lip between his teeth.

Her hands moved on his shirtfront, absorbing the man within the warm, silky fabric. She could hear her own gasping breaths, her own fluttering, overfast heartbeat. The curling heat and sexual aches in her body were becoming unbearable.

Cooper's mouth moved to the hollow of her throat. His breath and lips were moist and hot. Kate's head went back, her eyelids drifting shut, and she wove her fingers into his hair.

She was reeling, Kate knew. Her legs were trembling and not very cooperative. She thought of how bold it would sound to mention her bedroom, but she couldn't continue to stand there.

"Cooper...please..."

He heard, and understood, and Kate was swept up off the floor. "Upstairs?"

"No. Granddad's old study."

In the flurry of lifting her, the skirt of Kate's dress had swirled. Cooper's hand resided on her bare behind, and the thought of Kate's warm, silken body without underwear hastened his long strides to the room she had indicated.

A lamp burned beside the bed. Cooper took only one swift glance around the room that had once been Les Redmond's private domain. He heard the radio playing, but only vaguely. He let Kate's feet slide to the floor, but didn't remove his hand from beneath her skirt.

The skin and the rounded flesh of her bottom seared his palm. A red haze of overwhelming desire was blurring Cooper's vision. He had to forcibly stop himself from finishing this quickly, from laying her on the bed, pushing up her skirt and unzipping his pants, from taking her with no further preliminaries. In a racing, searing thought he considered it, then ashamedly discarded it. He had too many special feelings for Kate to treat her so shabbily, feelings he was only beginning to recognize and wonder about, true. But understood or not, they were strong enough to prevent him from satisfying his own wildness and ignoring her needs.

That he could even have such a selfish, self-gratifying urge startled Cooper. It was something that had never happened to him before. He'd never, ever been so overcome by a woman that a loss of control had nearly made him forget everything else.

He drew a long, alarmed breath and concentrated on slowing down. This was going to be as good for Kate as he could make it, he vowed. This was not something to hurry through. Why had he even felt such haste?

Retreating from the exciting secrets beneath her skirt, he cupped her face with his hands. "You're so beautiful, Katie," he whispered, and softly kissed her lips.

Kate's heart was beating so fiercely it felt like a tom-tom in her chest. Cooper's kisses kept falling on her mouth, her cheeks, each feature of her face. Her fingertips traveled his jawline and then down into the collar of his shirt. They stopped at the first button and worked it open. And then the next, and the next, until she was at his belt.

Kate had seen Cooper's bare chest many times, and even discounting those occasions, a man's chest was no big deal, was it?

Cooper's was. Looking at the dark hair and the hard muscles within the opening of his shirt was like seeing a man's chest for the very first time for Kate. Her breath actually stopped for an intoxicated moment.

"You're beautiful, too," she whispered, and pressed her mouth to the pulse beat at the base of his throat. He smelled wonderful. Kate breathed in his scent and remembered that even when she'd been a mere girl, Cooper's scent had been unique and special to her.

She felt him searching her dress. "How does it open?"

"It doesn't. There's elastic at strategic spots. I have to take it off like this." Kate took one small backward step and slipped the straps of the dress down over her shoulders. Cooper's eyes were smoky and following her every movement. "See?" she said huskily, and began to push the top of the dress down.

"Let me."

She nodded. Cooper's trembling hands replaced hers on the top of the dress. He worked it down very slowly, mesmerized by the first sign of cleavage. Below a tan line, two ivory half moons, the tops of her breasts, appeared, and he stopped the dress's movement just short of her nipples.

His eyes were dark and partially hooded, Kate saw. Her breasts weren't large, but Cooper already knew that, and if the look on his face was any measure, he was seeing her body as perfect. Watching him admire her gave Kate a glorious feeling of utter and complete femaleness.

His gaze rose to her face. There was something so hot and sensual on its path, Kate threw every caution to the wind. Everything had changed so fast; their anger had erupted into this, into desire so strong she could barely breathe. And it felt so right. That's what stunned Kate, how right it felt. "Make love to me," she whispered.

That was why they were in this room with its bed

and soft lamplight. The knowledge was shared, having already been decided and accepted. But Kate saying it added another dimension to raw, ragged feelings.

The deceptive indolence Cooper had been practicing vanished like a puff of smoke. Kate's dress was dragged down in an almost harsh jerk and ended up in a colorful puddle around her feet. Dark blue eyes seared her nakedness while Cooper tore his shirt off, then went for his pants. His shoes were kicked aside, his socks with them. And, seemingly, all at once, he was as naked as Kate.

Her eyes traveled down his lean torso, down to the jutting maleness at the base of his tight belly. He was powerfully built, a perfection of male strength. The memory of that one long-ago night suddenly filled every nook and cranny of Kate's brain. She had been so astonished by it all, she remembered. She had never seen an adult male in arousal before, and certainly had never been the cause of such a mysterious—to her inexperienced eyes—process.

Kate felt similar feelings now, even though a man's body was no longer a mystery. But tonight's unleashed desire was the first time she had even come close to what she had felt that night by the river with Cooper. And she understood it now. Only with the man she loved would she ever feel such uninhibited passion. Only with Cooper.

Then, abruptly, there was no more staring, no more delay. They tumbled to the bed in each other's arms, eager to touch, to explore tactile sensation. Mouth kisses were stolen and greedy. Hands moved and searched and found erotic pleasures.

"Now," she moaned. "Now, Cooper."

His head came up. "Are you protected?"

Her eyes closed with a despairing sigh. "No."

"Kate, I don't have anything. I never thought..."
An oddly gleeful thought bubbled in his brain. She
wasn't on the Pill. She couldn't be very sexually active
in New York.

They were both silent a moment, digesting the risk
and the racking, aching desire gripping them. They
weren't going to stop; they couldn't. But they were
adults and knew the risk they would be taking.

Cooper's hand slid between her thighs, and she relaxed them, giving herself to him completely. His
mouth glided over her breasts, opening around an up-
right, turgid nipple. His fingers moved gently but
surely, driving Kate to another plateau of unrestrained
abandonment.

"Now," she repeated hoarsely, unable to lie still.
She would not get pregnant, she wouldn't, beat in her
brain. Or maybe she didn't care if she did. How could
she worry about practicality, about common sense,
when every inch of her body was on fire, when even
her skin felt tortured and demanded appeasement?

Kate urged Cooper into the cradle of her thighs. His
erection, his hot, hard maleness, pressed against the
opening of her body. His voice was ragged, low, guttural. "Katie, are you sure?" If he entered her, he
would hold nothing back. Crazy thoughts bounced
around in his feverish brain. If she should say no now,
maybe he wouldn't stop anyway. Maybe he wouldn't
be able to. Completion now was as necessary as
breathing.

But she didn't say no. "Don't talk," she whispered.
"Just love me."

The sound from his throat was half-growl, half-sigh
as he slid into her heat. "Oh, Katie, Katie." His hands

burrowed beneath her hips, lifting them, raising them to the best possible union.

And then, with his head beside hers on the same pillow, he began the intense plunges that would bring the rapture of release they both so desperately needed. Each thrust brought a sough from Kate. Their skin became dewy with perspiration, their breaths coming in short, rasping pants.

Kate's fingers moved on Cooper's damp back, her nails restlessly scoring, circling. He went deep into the hot tight corridor of her femininity, again and again. Over and over. The rhythm was steady for long, intensifying minutes.

And then the world began cracking for Kate. The aching knot of molten heat in her body began expanding, liquefying, spilling over into blindingly, excruciatingly pleasurable spasms. Tears formed and dripped from her eyes, while she clung to her lover and emitted cries of total submission.

It was what Cooper had been waiting for. Released from a teeth-gritting determination to satisfy Kate first, he moved faster and with all the pent-up, sexually charged energy in his body. His mind was soaring, sailing off to never-never land while his body exulted in the glory of Katie.

And then…it was over. The bed stopped creaking and rocking. The radio's music penetrated the silence of utter satisfaction, of a satiation of senses for both Cooper and Kate.

Lying beneath Cooper, Kate's ability to think slowly returned. Her interior felt soft and vulnerable. Too easily, at this moment, she could murmur something loving. She kept her eyes closed and her lips compressed tightly together, and the sheen of tears glistened on her lashes.

Things looked painfully clearer to her, why she hadn't handled the lawsuit in a businesslike way, why she had had to confront Cooper instead of hitting him with the normal legal process due such cases.

But how, dear God, how had she not known that she loved him before actually returning? There must have been clues within her own psyche. This wasn't a brand new feeling; it was merely the rebirth of what she had lived with before.

Leave now?

No, absolutely not. Nor would she give Cooper that document tonight. She wanted more than a summer affair with him. They had a long way to go. Kate was too realistic not to see the problems between them. If he should say right this minute that he was in love with her, the problems would still exist.

Making love like this without protection suddenly filled her mind. She should get up; she shouldn't lie here and bask in the warmth of his weight. But if she were pregnant, wouldn't that force him to…?

"My God," she mumbled, half ill at the deception of her thoughts. Trapping Cooper, or any other man, into marriage was a horrifying idea. "Let me get up."

Cooper raised his head. He looked wonderfully relaxed, no longer impatient, no longer tense, and he gave her a slow, lovely-to-look-at smile. "You're incredible."

Kate couldn't smile back. She might have been incredible a few minutes ago, but now she was only scared. "Let me up, please."

He kissed her lips. Kate's eyelids fluttered. It was difficult to maintain sensibility through this kind of intimacy. They were still joined, still lethargic with repletion, and Cooper's body was a sensuous, warm blanket over hers.

Touching his cheek, a gentle plea in the gesture, Kate moved her mouth aside. "I have to get up," she whispered.

Cooper finally understood. "Sorry, I forgot." When he'd moved away, Kate jumped up and bolted for the door.

While Kate was gone, an urge for a cigarette was like a physical pain for Cooper. He'd been doing so well without smoking. It had been weeks since his last cigarette, and he'd been thinking of the habit less and less.

But now, with the events of the day and then tonight, loving Kate and feeling her exhilarating response, the desire to light up was close to intolerable. It was a frustration he would have to bear; there wasn't a cigarette in miles.

They had to talk, Cooper knew. He'd learned nothing tonight from Kate, not why she was leaving, not what it was she had wanted to tell him before she went.

Crooking an elbow beneath his head, Cooper laid back against a pillow. She would tell him everything now, he decided with a satisfying sense of harmony. After the incredible togetherness they had just shared, there was no reason for her to hold anything back. They would speak as lovers now, without inhibitions, without reservations.

A yawn reminded Cooper of how tired he was. It didn't matter. He had to get on some sort of even keel with Kate yet tonight as he had to fly back to Reno first thing in the morning.

Hearing water running somewhere in the house, Cooper's lips turned up with a soft smile. Tonight had been more than special. He would like to make it last. There was no reason why he shouldn't spend the night right here with Kate. Then they could snuggle and murmur secrets to each other in the dark.

The word "secrets" gave him pause. His secrets weren't very clearly defined, were they? He'd been questioning his feelings for Kate even before this, but it was Kate's secrets he wanted to delve into. She was such a private woman. Even as a girl she hadn't been very talkative. Oh, she'd yelled and sworn with the best of them in anger, but she had rarely exposed her inner thoughts on any other level.

Her mother leaving her with Les and then virtually disappearing had been one subject Cooper had learned to avoid, he remembered now. To his eyes, Kate had not had an unhappy childhood. She had been close to her grandfather and in love with the valley. There had been a strange sort of kinship between Cooper and Kate in those days, a bond because of both being orphaned at tender ages and living with a grandfather.

Lying in Kate's bed now, though, Cooper recognized the differences of their pasts. His parents hadn't deliberately deserted him, while Kate had grown up knowing *her* parents, her mother especially, had done just that. That must have been very difficult for her, very painful, he mused, seeing a side of Kate's youth he hadn't really considered before.

A series of sharp raps at the back door brought Cooper off the bed with a start. Glancing at the bedroom doorway, expecting to see Kate on her way to see who was knocking, he grabbed his pants off the floor and yanked them on.

She must not have heard, Cooper decided as he made his way through the house. He opened the door to Dirk.

"Sorry to bother you, Coop, but Jack Leonard just called."

"An emergency?" Cooper sensed Dirk's awareness of his state of undress. Answering a woman's door barefoot and shirtless was pretty solid evidence of what had been going on. Something was wrong, however. Dirk hadn't come over here just for the hell of it.

"Jack wants you to call him right away." Dirk launched into a story that stiffened Cooper's spine. When he'd heard enough to get the gist of Jack's message, he growled, "Call Jack and tell him I'm on my way back to Reno."

"In the dark?"

Cooper had flown after dark enough to know he didn't like it. But it couldn't be helped tonight. "I'll be leaving in ten minutes." Nodding, Dirk sprinted away.

Cursing under his breath, Cooper slammed the door closed and made a harried dash, for the bedroom. He met Kate, wearing her pink robe in the hall. "I've got to leave." Brushing past her, he went into the bedroom and found his shirt.

Somewhat stunned, Kate leaned against the door frame. "That was Dirk at the door. What's wrong?"

"Some damned idiot tried to hold up the casino cage," Cooper replied angrily. "A security guard was shot in the leg and the would-be robber was shot, too.

All hell broke loose, with the customers screaming and running. I've got to get back right away.''

Kate digested the brief amount of startling information with a frown. She fought against selfishness, but she had hoped for so much more from the balance of this evening. "What can you do?" she asked quietly.

Cooper was tucking his shirt into his pants. "It's still my place, Kate. I'm the one to deal with the police and the publicity. I've probably got a hotel full of panicked guests to reassure." He sat on the bed to pull on his socks and shoes. "God, I'll be glad when Sinclair's becomes someone else's problem!"

It took a moment for the ardent but vague comment to sink in. Kate moved closer to the bed and Cooper. "Is it going to become someone else's problem?"

"What?" Cooper looked up. "Oh, yeah, I didn't mention that I'm selling the place, did I?"

Kate's pulse quickened. Cooper was obviously planning to live full-time in the valley again. The thought was instantly provocative, exciting. "No, you didn't."

Cooper stood up. He looked at Kate in her pink robe and thought of what he'd wanted from this night, the talking, the cuddling, the sharing of ideas and feelings.

The lovemaking.

Ah, yes, the lovemaking. A jolting conviction struck Cooper: he could make love to Kate again right this minute. His thoughts turned wry. Despite an indisputable weariness, he could "rise" to the occasion.

He shook his head. It would have to wait.

But…would Kate wait?

Cooper put his hands on her shoulders. "I hate going, but I have to. Will you be here when I come back?"

Kate searched the depths of Cooper's eyes. What was she seeing? she wondered with some uneasiness and very little, confidence. Affection? Possession? "When...?" She hesitated, then completed the question. "When will you be back?"

"I don't know. But we have to talk. Will you call me tomorrow?"

"From your ranch?"

"If there was a phone here, I'd call you."

Picturing herself hanging around the Sinclair ranch to connect with Cooper by telephone wasn't a pleasant exercise. "What time should I try to reach you?"

Cooper, too, saw the probable hurdles. Sinclair's was probably a madhouse tonight. He should have been there, which was no doubt going to double, even triple, the demands on his time when he got back. The press, the TV newspeople, the Gaming Commission, the police, and last, but certainly not least, the injured security guard were all going to require a great deal of his personal attention.

His hands were tied. He had no choice but to go and unravel the mess, although he'd give anything he owned to be able to stay right here with Kate tonight.

"Ah, Katie," he breathed in unhappy resignation, and drew her head to his chest. "Just promise you won't leave without seeing me again. Can you do that?"

The note of desperation in Cooper's voice raised Kate's hopes. Maybe she *was* important to him. Dear God, if she was...

"I'll be here when you come back," she said softly. His arms squeezed around her in response.

"I'll get back as soon as I can." Cooper tilted her chin then. His lips brushed hers. "At least *try* to call me, all right?"

Kate nodded, and then Cooper was gone. She followed his long, quick strides through the house and felt his anxiety. He had to go; she understood that. At the door he kissed her again, but Kate was positive his mind was no longer on her. She understood that, too, even if it did leave her feeling rather forlorn.

Locking the door behind him, Kate switched off the kitchen light and listened to Cooper drive away. When everything was quiet, she slowly walked back to her bedroom.

Nine

Cooper received the shock of his life when he walked into Sinclair's and saw business as usual. The table games were crowded, the slot-players were yanking handles at maximum speed, and the country band within the Maverick Saloon was blaring its music through immense speakers and filling every small cell of possible quiet in the din with guitars and drum beats.

He'd expected chaos, possibly even the casino being shut down, but not this. If anything, business was even brisker than normal. Not that the casino closed its doors often. Only one time had Sinclair's casino been silent and lifeless since its grand opening: the day of Sam Sinclair's funeral.

Absorbing the action on the first floor from his office balcony, Cooper went through a series of emotions, the most disturbing of which was a realization that he hadn't had to leave Kate tonight. Apparently Jack had handled the incident as well as *he* could have. Granted, a lot could be accomplished in a couple of hours, the length of time it had taken Cooper to fly back to Reno. Nearly three hours of cautious, after-dark procedure, to be scrupulously accurate. But all during the flight, Cooper had worried.

Obviously his concern had been wasted energy.

It was after midnight. The administration offices were empty except for a handful of night employees. Jack had gone home, and the night casino manager had everything under control. There really wasn't one thing that needed special attention tonight. It gave Cooper a weird, disconnected feeling.

But then his expression cleared. There was one thing he *wanted* to do. Entering his office, Cooper flipped through the telephone directory, then dialed the hospital. After hearing the injured security guard was doing fine, Cooper left his office and pointed himself at the elevator. He was exhausted. He also felt deeply, gnawingly unsettled. Too tired to sort out his mixed feelings, he went into his fifth floor suite, undressed and fell into bed.

Kate could not go to sleep. A few minutes of exquisite lovemaking did not ensure emotional tranquility, she realized during long hours of restlessness. Quite the contrary. She had fallen even deeper in love with Cooper, and, consequently, given herself an increased burden to bear. Telling herself to be mature and worldly about tonight was futile; she *wasn't* worldly about sex with Cooper, and that was that.

As for maturity, well, that was another ball game.

She was at a time of life, and so was Cooper, where relationships went somewhere.

But where could a relationship between Les Redmond's and Sam Sinclair's grandkids go?

That old battle still had to be fought, didn't it? Or, at least, talked about? Picked apart? Dissected and digested? The contention that had existed between Sam and Les was, sadly, a part of the present, like it or not.

Kate's battles that night were with fantasies, however, not with Sam and Les. She didn't want to picture Cooper and her living in the valley together, but she did. She tried not to see the two of them happily, lovingly married and having babies, but the vision haunted her every time she closed her eyes.

Cooper selling Sinclair's was earthshaking news. Mustang Valley was taking on new meaning again. With Cooper living there full-time, the valley would be like it used to be. The one image Kate didn't try to dispel was of her and Cooper riding together, through grassy, sun-drenched fields and following trails into the mountains.

And there was no way to block out tonight. No matter how many times Kate punched her pillow or turned over in bed to seek an apparently impossible-to-attain comfort, tonight remained the high point of her adult life. For a few minutes she and Cooper had been on exactly the same wavelength. Kate continued to feel those minutes, to savor them, even though reliving them brought tears to her eyes.

It hurt to think she could be reaching for the stars and that Cooper might see their lovemaking as just another affair. Some people could be very emotional in an affair without intending anything permanent, Kate knew.

She would remain in an emotionally painful limbo until Cooper returned, Kate concluded on a long, soulful sigh.

And, with all that was going on in Reno, that could be for days and days.

At first light Cooper awoke. The second his eyes opened, yesterday came flooding back in a mishmash of disjointed memories—Kate—his decision to sell Sinclair's—the insane episode of the attempted robbery—the obviously excellent manner in which Jack had reacted.

When everything just kept swirling around in his brain, Cooper threw back the covers and got up. Pulling on a pair of red shorts, a short-sleeved T-shirt and his running shoes, he left his suite, rode the elevator down to the first floor and exited the hotel-casino by its private side door.

Reno's sidewalks were all but deserted, containing only a few weary, all-night gamblers, or those that rose early to hit the machines before the crowds gathered. Cooper did his normal stretching exercises, then started off at an easy lope.

Sometimes he really enjoyed running, and this morning it felt particularly good. Cooper never ran with a radio in his ears, as so many people did, much preferring his own thoughts to canned music. While his muscles worked and his blood pumped harder, he could actually feel the cool morning air clearing the cobwebs from his brain.

Kate was a primary concern. He'd left her too soon and too abruptly after their lovemaking. She'd promised to stay until he got back to the valley, but he keenly suspected she wouldn't wait for very long. He had to get back to her before she took the notion to head for New York.

What had seemed so important to her yesterday on the phone and then, apparently, been unspeakable last night? In some ways, Kate was maddening. Grinning as he ran, Cooper admitted that she had been maddening years ago, too, as stubborn and headstrong then as she was now.

But damn, she was deeply embedded in his system! What was he going to do about that, kiss her again, then wave her off to New York?

The idea created a cold knot in Cooper's belly. He and Kate had a strange connection, one born in the past, influenced by their grandfathers and too strong to ignore today.

He thought of last night, the soft arms around him, the beautiful, sexy mouth opened to his, the silky hair and skin, the heat and scent of femaleness. Kate was an extraordinarily passionate and uninhibited woman in bed. Physically they communicated perfectly, and just thinking about it gave Cooper an overwhelming sense of Kate's drawing power. He couldn't let her leave.

But how could he persuade her to stay?

Would a marriage proposal do it?

Cooper emitted a confused snort. Kate would probably regress to the shouting, cussing girl she'd been if he even hinted at marriage between them. Great sex didn't necessarily involve emotions, and he really had no clues to Kate's private feelings. She wanted old Les's land back, that was really the only thing he knew about Kate with any degree of certainty.

Kate and those blasted water rights weren't his only problems, either. If he was going to sell Sinclair's, it was time to get that show on the road. And just what part of his ego had been making him think he was so damned indispensable around the casino? He'd rushed back, even flying after dark, when he recalled very clearly now that Dirk had merely relayed Jack's request for a telephone call.

By the time Cooper completed his usual three-mile circuit and ended up back at Sinclair's, he had a few brand new ideas. After ordering breakfast in his suite, he showered, shaved and dressed. His cereal and coffee were delivered, and he ate quickly, eager to get to work.

Then he went down to his office. He had an hour yet before the regular staff arrived for the day, and he pulled out a yellow pad of paper and began writing.

To elude senseless pacing and worrying, Kate took Shadow out for a long ride. When she returned to the house, she dawdled through a bath and a manicure. The few daily chores in a one-woman establishment took little time, more's the pity, she thought wryly while applying a coat of pink polish to her nails. She didn't have enough to do to mentally steer clear of Cooper, and his image had ridden with her earlier and was with her now.

Sighing, Kate forced her thoughts to the telephone call she had promised Cooper last night. Odds were, no matter what time of day she placed the call, Cooper would be busy with some phase of Sinclair's operation and away from his desk. It seemed rather fruitless to her to drive over to his ranch just to hear that he was unavailable from his secretary.

Facing Dirk might be uncomfortable, too. Although Dirk certainly wasn't a giggly teenager, Kate had a lifelong aversion to other people knowing her private business. And there was no way Dirk wouldn't have figured out that his boss and Kate Redmond had been in bed together when he'd knocked on the door last night.

The whole situation just didn't set right with Kate. She didn't want to see masculine amusement in Dirk's eyes, and the possibility of Cooper's secretary asking her to wait at the ranch until Cooper called her back was even more discomfiting.

At three, Kate got in her car and drove the twenty miles to the small town where she purchased her groceries. She bought a few things, then forced herself into a public telephone booth.

Exactly as she'd thought, Cooper was tied up. His secretary added, after that announcement, "But he told me to expect your call, Miss Redmond. His meeting shouldn't last more than another hour, and he will call you back."

"No, I won't be at a phone. Please give him a message for me."

"Certainly."

"Tell him..." Kate stopped. Tell him what? That she loved him, but she hated calling him like this? That she would be in the valley when he returned, but she wasn't going to hang around his ranch waiting for a call back?

"Just tell him I called."

"Well, yes, but..."

"Thank you." Kate put the phone on the hook with a sad, sinking sensation. The distance between her and Cooper was more than mere miles. She would wait, as she'd promised, until he came back to the valley, but she couldn't help being unhappy about the interminable waiting. It seemed to Kate that waiting was what she had done the most of since she'd returned to Nevada.

Driving home, Kate reminded herself of her own decision to stay, which she'd reached even before Cooper had mentioned it. But that had also been before he had dashed off at the first sign of trouble in Reno.

Well, the trouble *had* been serious, Kate admitted with wry self-castigation. She could hardly take offense or claim desertion because Cooper had felt so compelled to get back to Reno under those circumstances.

It was tough to deal with the kind of helplessness distance instilled, though, even approaching the subject with common sense. Kate completed the drive with a dejected expression.

Cooper came out of the conference room and headed directly to his own office. He stopped at Kathy's desk. "Did she call?"

The young woman nodded. "About an hour and a half ago. But you can't call her back. She said she wouldn't be at a phone."

"Why not?" Cooper's forehead was crisscrossed with a heavy frown.

"She didn't explain."

"Nothing?"

"I'm sorry, Cooper."

Perplexed, Cooper acknowledged Kathy's empathy with a rather absent "Forget it. It's not your fault." He went on into his office and closed the door. The meeting had gone so well, and he'd left it in high spirits. But he had to talk to Kate and tell her he wouldn't be back in the valley for another week. Just one week, and then he'd be there permanently.

God, the thought was mind-boggling, incredible, wonderful, euphoric. Of course, until Sinclair's actually belonged to a new owner, he would have to make periodic visits to Reno. But Jack Leonard had been delighted to take over full management during the interim. Jack's opinion, which made sense to Cooper, too, was that the new owner would better understand Jack's capabilities if he'd been operating the hotel-casino as its chief executive officer.

The arrangement would help Jack's future with the operation and free Cooper, and both men knew that even if a buyer came along tomorrow, the paperwork could take months.

Jack had asked for only one week of Cooper's time. "Not that I don't understand your duties, Coop. But let's make sure of every detail, okay?"

There had been a lot of people at that meeting. Announcing his retirement plans and Jack's promotion had involved every person in administration, Cooper's attorney, Dave Walker, and a high-ranking member of the Nevada Gaming Commission.

Cooper felt that everything was smoothing out in Reno. But Kate's apparent nonchalance about talking to him by telephone was a definitely discordant note in the day's satisfying events.

He dialed the ranch and got Leila. "Does Kate still happen to be there, Leila?"

"Kate? She hasn't been here today, Coop. Was she supposed to be?"

"We, uh, mentioned it. Don't worry about it. Is Dirk around?"

"Dirk went to Carson City to pick up that new part

for the tractor he ordered last week. Do you want him to call you when he gets back?''

''He can try, but I'm going to be busy. I'll catch him tonight.''

Cooper put the phone down and anxiously raked his fingers through his hair. In the next instant he began searching his desk drawers. He would quit smoking again when he was living in the valley. Right now, Kate was driving him crazy, and he couldn't deal with her and not smoking, too.

''Kathy!'' he yelled.

She stuck her head in the door. ''Yes?''

''Have someone bring me up a pack of cigarettes.''

''Cooper!''

Kathy's disgusted expression didn't even register. ''You know my brand. Tell whoever you get to bring them up to step on it.''

Kate answered her door reluctantly. She'd seen Dirk driving in and knew very well he was delivering a message from Cooper. Kate wanted to hear the message; Dirk, she could do without.

''Evenin', Kate.''

''Hello, Dirk.''

''Cooper asked me to come and drive you over to the ranch. He's waiting on the phone.''

''He's *waiting* on the phone, long distance?''

''Yep.''

Kate took a peek into Dirk's dark eyes and felt relief that she saw nothing different than she always had. If the man had any amused thoughts about last night, he was keeping them to himself. She felt like patting him on the back, but Cooper waiting in Reno for her to answer his call took precedence over the urge.

This looked serious, Kate thought with sudden breathtaking elation. Cooper really wanted to maintain contact.

Stepping out on the porch, Kate pulled the door closed behind her. "Let's go," she exclaimed.

Seated in Dirk's pickup truck, they sped toward the Sinclair house. "I saw you on Shadow again this morning," Dirk commented. "You ride real well, Kate."

"Thanks. I love riding."

"You grew up in Mustang Valley, just like Cooper."

"Yes."

"On that hundred acres?"

Dirk didn't know the story. How strange. Leila had to remember what happened ten years ago. How odd that she hadn't passed it on.

Kate sighed and avoided the brunt of the old tale. "In that same house, Dirk. It was my grandfather's house."

"Is he still living?"

"No."

"Too bad. Coop talks about Sam sometimes. He sounds like quite a character. I wish I'd met him. Do you remember Sam?"

"Like the back of my hand," Kate mumbled, feeling again the old resentments, the old hostilities. They startled her. She'd become so preoccupied with Cooper, Sam's cunning, his chicanery, had been pushed aside. But deciding to give Cooper the water rights for her own peace of mind had merely diminished the memory of Sam's sins, not eradicated them, Kate uneasily realized.

The whole situation with Cooper and the valley was

becoming terribly convoluted. She'd recognized the differences of her and Cooper's opinions and feelings toward their respective grandfathers, and that those feelings were not merely trivial facets of an extremely complex relationship. But a major showdown on the two old men could destroy the gains she and Cooper had made this summer. Even those intensely meaningful strides made last night.

Kate felt an internal division. During last night's restlessness she'd seen a necessary battle brewing between her and Cooper on the past, but tonight, just the thought of it made her queasy.

Dirk stopped in the Sinclair driveway. "The phone in the study is off the hook."

"Thanks." Kate jumped out of the pickup and hurried into the house. In Cooper's own study, she grabbed up the receiver. "Hello, Cooper."

"Hello, Katie."

He sounded so far away. Kate sank down on the chair behind the desk. "How are you?"

"Wishing you were here. Or, better yet, that I was there."

This was no time for vacillation or anything cute, Kate knew. "I wish you were here, too," she replied softly.

"Do you, Kate? We don't communicate very well when we're together, do we?"

"Not verbally, Cooper."

"We communicated very well in each other's arms last night, though, didn't we?"

"Yes," she whispered, reliving every moment of last night in one speeding, searing flash of memory. Flushed, Kate cleared her throat. "I'm sorry I didn't reach you today."

"Where did you call from?"

"A pay phone."

"You drove to a pay phone rather than go to the ranch."

"It seemed best—at the time."

Cooper released a long breath. There were things about Kate he might never understand. "I can't come back to the valley for a week."

A week. Kate chewed her bottom lip. Another week of waiting.

"Say something," Cooper said quietly.

She stole a breath. "I'll be here."

"Kate, are you sure?"

"I'll be here, Cooper."

Cooper was using a cordless phone and pacing from one end of his suite to the other while he talked. Recalling Kate being here that one time gave him an exciting idea. "Something just occurred to me. I can't leave for another week, but you could come here, Kate."

"To Reno?"

"Why didn't I think of this before? Yes, Kate, to Reno. I'll be busy a great deal of the time, but we can have most evenings together. I've got a lot to tell you. I was going to talk about it on the phone, but I'd much rather tell you in person. Say you'll come. I'll have the helicopter pick you up in the morning."

The lawsuit suddenly weighted Kate's mind, maybe because that's what had brought her to Reno before. She hated thinking about it at this point, but just how far would Cooper really go to hang onto complete ownership of Mustang Valley?

Maybe he had already gone the long mile. Maybe

last night, and now this invitation to Reno were merely…

Oh, dear Lord! Stop it, just stop it! When had she become so insecure? So suspicious? She was normally a competent, thinking, intelligent woman.

And fearing Cooper in any way, either because he loved her or because he didn't, whatever his motives might be, was ludicrous and becoming more so every day!

Kate gathered her wits. "I'll come, Cooper. I'm looking forward to it." She heard Cooper's swift intake of air.

He sounded jubilant. "Honey, you won't be sorry. We'll have a great week together, I promise. We've got a lot of talking to do. There are some very exciting things going on here right now."

"Yes, we do have a lot of talking to do."

"And a lot of loving?"

Kate's heart took a crazy leap. There was a teasing note in Cooper's voice, but there was a promise and a challenge in it, too. He did plan on the week being extremely intimate, she realized, and if she objected at all, now was the time to say so.

Lord, if this really was only an affair to Cooper, she was letting herself in for some terrible heartache. Smiling bravely, Kate murmured, "You sound rather anxious."

Cooper's husky voice whispered in her ear. "I am anxious. I wish you were here tonight. Katie, I'm not sure I understand you and everything that's going on between us, but I have no doubts about wanting you. Does that make any kind of sense to you?"

It struck Kate that Cooper was either an incredible actor or was truly undergoing an emotional struggle.

Was it possible he was really falling in love with her and having trouble recognizing the feeling for what it was?

The thought was warming, accurate or not. And could she really blame his confusion, if that were the case? Wasn't she equally as confused about their relationship?

You're not confused about your love for Cooper, a small voice in Kate's head reminded. Which was true. But every other aspect of their relationship was troubling and certainly unclear.

"It makes some sense," she conceded. "I can't deny my participation in last night, Cooper."

"No, I didn't think you would. It was wonderful, Kate. There's only one other evening in my life that compares. Do you know which one I mean?"

Her words were shaky. "That night by the river?"

"That night by the river," Cooper softly concurred. "Know what I want to do when we get back to the valley after this week?"

A low laugh bubbled from Kate's throat. "I think I'm getting an idea."

"Are you game?"

A spurt of Kate's usual spirit prompted a rather sassy, "I'm game for anything you are, Mr. Sinclair."

He chuckled. "We'll just see about that, Miss Redmond. My imagination's been running wild all day."

"So has mine," she whispered.

"What time do you want the helicopter in the morning?"

"Around ten should do it."

"I'll see you around noon, then. And Katie, if I'm tied up, just make yourself at home. I'll have you shown to my suite. Order from room service, or just sign the check in any of the restaurants. Sinclair's is yours for the week, honey.''

Kate drew a deep breath. ''That sounds…fine. I'll see you tomorrow. Good night, Cooper.''

Ten

It was a strange sensation to be alone in Cooper's suite. Kate had been escorted to the fifth floor with her luggage and a message that Mr. Sinclair sent a greeting and an apology: he was in a meeting.

The luggage still sat near the door and seemed to be confronting Kate every time she looked at it. She wasn't comfortable in this spacious, beautifully decorated suite, even though she had agreed to the trip. But this was so blatantly Cooper's turf, and accepting his invitation was so…so what? Inane? Hasty? Risky?

Kate searched her mind and emotions and recognized the symptoms of intense stress. She was ill-at-ease, walking the floor and becoming sorry she'd followed her heart. Yes, she wanted to further a relationship that was, in all honesty, just getting off the ground. But was moving in with Cooper for a week the best way to accomplish that?

"Damn!" she muttered, and finding herself very close to her suitcases, Kate gave the nearest one a sharp kick. Yes, this had definitely been a hasty decision. And maybe inane wasn't a completely appropriate adjective for what she was doing, but risky certainly was!

The sound of the key in the lock alerted Kate, jangling every nerve in her body. She ran over to the sofa and faced the door, arranging her features into as sedate an expression as she could manage. Cooper walked in, his eyes lighting up when he saw her. He quickly closed the door. "They told me you were here. I'm sorry..."

"Don't apologize, please! I know you're busy." Kate sidestepped the arms that reached out to her.

Cooper stopped and studied her. Kate was stunning in a raspberry silk pantsuit and high heels. Her two suitcases were proof of her intention to spend the week here, but eluding his embrace was evidence that all was not well.

Also, she had been in the suite for at least an hour, and it was pretty obvious she hadn't moved from this one room.

"Did you have lunch?" he asked quietly.

"I wasn't...I'm *not* hungry."

Cooper swung away and went over to the phone. "Well, I am." He ordered crab salad, toasted sourdough bread and coffee for two from room service, keeping Kate's nervous indifference in view all the while.

After last night's telephone conversation, he hadn't expected Kate to be either nervous *or* indifferent today. All morning, behind meetings and the business he'd had to attend to had been the thought of Kate on her way to Reno. He'd been sure she would have unpacked and ordered herself some lunch when he hadn't been here at noon, and, apparently, all she had done was stand there and regret coming.

That's what he saw in the rigid thrust of her shoulders, and in the green eyes that wouldn't quite meet his, regret. Why? What had happened now to change her mood so drastically?

Kate's unease was catching. Suddenly uncomfortable himself, Cooper tried to appear otherwise. He took off his suit jacket and folded it over the back of a chair. "Sit down," he invited.

Kate hesitated, then perched on the edge of a chair. Her efforts to look calm and unshook worked much better when she forced herself deeper into the chair. But she wasn't much of an actress, she realized with an inner wince when her voice came out sounding hard and unfriendly. "This is a mistake, Cooper."

He sat down and smiled wryly, spreading his arms along the top of the sofa. "Now, how did I know that's what you were thinking?"

Their gazes dueled for a lengthy stretch. Kate felt awful. This was all wrong. She hadn't meant to sound cold, and Cooper was taking her unintentional tone as a challenge. "I don't want to get into an argument," Kate finally declared, unable to prolong the staring contest any further.

"And you think I do? Kate, when I look at you, arguing is the farthest thing from my mind."

Ignoring the sensual ripple in his voice, Kate replied only to the literal sense of his words. She was confused and trying to sort things out, and again sounded distant. "We agree on one thing, at least."

Cooper raised an eyebrow. "Only one?"

He was baiting her. Kate told herself to remain cool, that Cooper might say anything at this point. He probably wasn't used to disappointment, to someone changing his plans like this. Just from the expensive elegance of this suite alone, anyone could figure out that Cooper Sinclair was used to getting just about anything he wanted.

Sam Sinclair had been used to the same way of life.

At the thought of Sam, Kate's eyes grew frosty, an involuntary reaction to old memories. "Can you think of another?"

"As a matter of fact, I can."

He looked amused now, which irritated Kate. He was referring to their lovemaking, she knew, which seemed damned presumptuous to her. It was a sad state of affairs to realize she was really *very* sorry she had come.

There was a solution to this mess, though. Kate raised her chin. "Is there a vacant room in the hotel?"

Cooper took a long moment to consider the question. "Is it safe to surmise that you're willing to stay, only not in this suite?"

"I think that's a…safe assumption, yes." Her hesitant answer surprised her, but only for a second. She still wanted time with Cooper, just not in this way. Not living together with every employee in the place knowing about it. Maybe she was a little too stiff-necked, but privacy in personal matters was important to Kate and not something she could turn on and off like a light bulb.

Besides, who really knew how this was going to turn out? Maybe they would both be glad to be able to retreat to separate quarters after some time together.

Cooper rose slowly. "Different floor, too?"

"Do I hear a note of sarcasm in that question?" Kate got to her feet, also.

"Don't get your hackles up. If I projected sarcasm, it's only because you've got me going in circles. You have a knack for that, Kate. Just when I think things are going well between us, you pull the rug out." Cooper walked over to the phone, picked it up and punched three buttons. "Hal? Cooper. I need a room on the fifth floor. What's available?"

Moving across the room, Kate stood at a window and looked down. She folded her arms and pretended interest in the street below, when her every sense was keenly attuned to Cooper's conversation.

"Five forty-eight? Fine. Have someone deliver the key to my suite. Thanks, Hal." The phone was put down. "Your room will be at the other end of the hall."

Kate turned. "Thank you."

Another long silence threatened. Kate's regrets expanded to include Cooper's disappointment. She hadn't started out to play this sort of game with him. She knew now that she should have heeded the niggling doubts gnawing at her while she packed and prepared for the trip.

But she really had wanted—*did* want—time with Cooper.

Kate moved to the sofa and stood beside it, one hand absently stroking its fine velveteen fabric. "I'm sorry," she said, giving him an oblique look. "I think I'm going in circles, too."

She saw some of the tension leave Cooper's shoulders, and then he smiled and walked over to her. His fingertips slid along her jaw, then up her cheek. Kate suddenly felt choked, but she didn't back away from his touch this time. "Katie, Katie, what's going on with us?" Cooper murmured softly.

A faint, tentative smile flickered across her lips. "I can't answer that."

"You can't or you won't? Do you *have* an answer?"

His eyes were so very blue, narrowed slightly in speculation. Looking into them, Kate wished she had the courage necessary for complete honesty. But until their relationship progressed—*if* it did—into something more solid, she was afraid to expose her feelings.

"I have only conjecture, Cooper, the same as you."

His fingers threaded into her hair while his gaze held hers. A kiss was in his eyes. Intimacy, too. Kate's breath nearly stopped. "I desire you, Kate, more than I've ever wanted any woman. What do you suppose that means?"

"What do *you* suppose it means?" she whispered.

He kept looking at her, probingly, searchingly. "That's what I've been trying to figure out."

A rat-a-tat at the door intruded. "That's probably lunch," Cooper said, leaving Kate and walking to the door. Her knees began trembling the moment Cooper's back was turned. They were getting very close to an extremely serious subject, and the thought was as jarring as it was welcome.

A service cart was wheeled in by a young man in a white jacket. He and Cooper chatted while the waiter set the table with linen, china, silver and the food Cooper had ordered. Before that task was completed, another man appeared with a set of keys to room 548.

In minutes Kate and Cooper were alone again. He pushed a button on a wall panel and lovely, muted music filled the suite. Then he pulled a chair away from the table. "Join me, Kate."

"Yes, thank you," she said huskily, ashamed of her previous curtness about lunch. Cooper spooned some crab salad onto her plate, then his, and sat across the table from her. "Toast?" he inquired, holding a basket out to her.

"Thank you."

After filling their cups with coffee, Cooper began eating. Kate picked up her fork and took a bite. "It's very good," she remarked with a glance across the table.

Cooper smiled. "What made you decide to study law, Kate?"

He was trying to put her at ease, Kate realized, and gratefully allowed her thoughts to leave this room, to go back to those days when she'd been in college and indecisive about a major. "Friends, actually. Late night dormitory conversations and countless talks over coffee at the local hangout, where everyone was guessing and wondering about the future. I considered teaching for a while, but then some statistician came up with data about a glut of teachers."

Kate smiled dryly. "The year I graduated law school, the statistics had shifted to the educational system turning out too many attorneys."

"Did you have trouble finding a position?"

"No, I was lucky. I was recruited even before graduation."

"Good grades, huh?"

"I made good grades, but frankly, I feel it also had something to do with the women's movement. Many traditionally all-male firms were actively seeking female law graduates."

"Do you like your work?"

Kate took a sip of coffee before answering. "What I like is the concept of law and order, Cooper. The idealism one gains in school is quickly shattered by the reality of practice. The caricature of a bleary-eyed attorney poring over mountains of law books, or writing long, dull briefs until the wee hours isn't all that exaggerated. Corporation law, which is what my firm specializes in, is pretty dry stuff most of the time. We also handle some civil litigation."

Civil litigation encompassed lawsuits such as Kate was threatening over Mustang Valley's water rights. Cooper noticed but ignored the connection. "Then you don't handle criminal cases at all?"

"I have no experience in criminal law. Speaking of which, how did that episode with the attempted robbery turn out?"

"The man is under police guard in the hospital. He was shot in the shoulder by a security guard, whom he had shot first. According to Jack and every other employee in the place I talked to, it was pure pandemonium in the casino for a few minutes."

"I can well imagine. Was the security guard badly injured?"

"Any bullet wound is serious business, but he's coming along fine."

"I'm glad to hear that."

Cooper smiled. "Something good came out of the incident, Kate, something I couldn't possibly have anticipated." He sat back with a pleased expression. "Have I ever mentioned Jack Leonard to you?"

Kate shook her head. "I don't recall the name."

"Well, Jack has been my right hand around here for years. The other night, he..." Cooper detailed

Jack's excellent control of the unfortunate affair, touting his tactful, intelligent approach with the news media, the police and especially with Sinclair's customers.

"It made me realize something, Kate. I've tied myself to this place unnecessarily. Sinclair's is up for sale, but anyone in the business knows how complex the transfer of gaming properties can be. The process could take months, and I don't want to be here that long."

Kate stared. "I'm not sure I follow you."

Cooper's smile broadened. "Jack's taking over as C.E.O. He knows the business inside out, but he asked for one week of my time to make absolutely sure he's missed nothing."

"Thus, the week you talked about last night on the phone," Kate said softly.

"And then I'm gone."

"To the valley."

"Exactly. I'm going to do what I've always wanted to do, stay in the valley and raise cattle." Cooper leaned forward. His eyes were alive and excited, a brilliant, dancing blue. "I feel like a kid with his first bicycle."

Kate smiled. "I can see that. I'm glad for you."

"Thanks." Sobering, Cooper said quietly, "Maybe that brings us to you, Kate."

"Me?"

"Or maybe we shouldn't get into that today," Cooper murmured.

A frown tautened Kate's features, and she dropped her eyes to her plate. He was referring to the lawsuit, a subject that gave her a sudden chill. They were not equally informed on the matter. She knew exactly what she was going to do about the water rights, but Cooper was still living with the agreement she had made with him to do nothing until Labor Day.

If she told him now that not only was the suit a dead issue for her, but that she had already drawn up a legal conveyance of water rights ownership, what would he say?

Kate's speculation was interrupted by the telephone. "Excuse me," Cooper said, getting up from the table.

When was she going to tell him? Kate asked herself while Cooper answered the phone. Was she really that afraid of what he might do or say? Did some part of her still believe he was being attentive only to dull her determination to sue him?

He was so incredibly handsome, Kate's heart beat faster just looking at him. His expression was serious and reflecting the content of his conversation. His tall, lean form, clothed today in pale gray pants and shirt with a navy and gray tie, was a sight Kate knew she would never tire of.

She wanted a future with Cooper; she *didn't* want to return to New York and spend the rest of her life trying to get over him.

For some reason Kate's thoughts turned to Dirk's ignorance of the Redmond-Sinclair feud. It seemed important, somehow.

"I'll be there in ten minutes," Cooper said into the phone with a finality that ended the conversation. He came back to the table and sat down. "I've got to go."

Their eyes met across the table, a moment heavy with contained sparks and unspoken feelings. "You're sure about the other room?" Cooper asked softly. It was on his face that he was hoping she had changed her mind, Kate saw.

She almost relented. Lunch had alleviated a lot of their tension, hers especially. But still, she would rather wait for Cooper in impersonal surroundings. And she also preferred having a place to go should things get too disturbing between them. "I think it's best." Kate hesitated, then spoke again, "Cooper, I'd like to ask you something. It will only take a minute."

Kate's determination was disheartening. Lunch had gone so well, and he'd hoped...

Well, so be it. She would still be very nearby. "Certainly. What is it?"

"When Dirk drove me to your ranch last night, we talked a little. He doesn't know what happened ten years ago, does he?"

Of all the questions Kate could have asked, this one puzzled Cooper. "I really don't know. *I've* never discussed it with him, but someone could have, I suppose."

"Leila could have."

"And it's bothering you that she didn't?"

What *was* bothering her about the incident? Kate wasn't sure herself, but it seemed rather sad that once the Redmonds left the valley, everyone simply forgot them. The old house standing in the middle of that fenced-in, dried-up hundred acres hadn't even been worthy of gossip.

Sighing, Kate laid her napkin beside her plate and stood up. "It's not important. Forget I even mentioned it. I know you've got work to do."

Cooper pushed himself up, a residue of perplexity on his face. "I'll carry your luggage down the hall."

"That's really not necessary. I can manage just fine."

Disregarding her protest, Cooper put his suit coat

on, then strolled to the suitcases and picked them up. "Bring the keys. They're on the coffee table."

Kate gathered her purse and the keys. They left Cooper's suite and traversed the long corridor in silence. Kate unlocked the door with 548 on it and entered first. It was a suite, too, she saw immediately. Not as grand as Cooper's, but comfortable and appealing all the same.

Cooper carried the luggage into the bedroom. Kate deposited her purse and the keys on a table and stayed in the sitting room until he reappeared. "Thank you."

He walked over to her. "You're not going to disappear this afternoon, are you?"

"No, of course not."

Her reply couldn't have been faster or more straightforward, but Cooper still wondered. Kate was still waters, and still waters ran deep. That thing about Dirk, for example. What did Kate see in such a trivial incident that he didn't?

Moving closer, Cooper touched her cheek. A tender protectiveness came over him. Kate hid her vulnerability so well, but she had it, the same as anyone else. "We'll have dinner together, all right?"

"Yes, that would be nice."

Cooper's gaze roamed her face. "I'm not sure what time I'll be back."

Kate forced a laugh, albeit a shaky one. Cooper's nearness, the graze of his fingertips, his scent, were doing predictable things to her system. "I'll be here," she promised.

He had no choice but to believe her. His body was stirring because of touching Kate, and standing here like this was inflicting fruitless discomfort upon himself. But more and more Kate was becoming a necessity, which, to Cooper, was a jolting realization. Needing Kate could be very risky business.

But she wouldn't be here if she didn't have some feelings for him, would she? With Kate, he just didn't know. She was strong-minded and guarded, selfish with her emotions. Even more so than she'd been years ago. Then, at least, he'd been able to tease her to anger. If he tried that now, the result wouldn't be funny, as it had been then.

No, he didn't want to get Kate angry. He'd had enough of anger between them. What he wanted from Kate was...

Cooper swallowed hard. Almost brusquely he lowered his head and pressed his lips to hers. The kiss was rampant with confusion and not very kind, startling Kate into wide-eyed breathlessness.

It lasted only a moment, then Cooper spun away. With a slanted glance at Kate, he picked up one of the room keys off of the table and walked to the door. "See you later," he announced unsmilingly.

Kate stared long after the door had closed behind him. Her heart was thudding with a strange foreboding. Cooper had made no threats, issued no ultimatums. But she had sensed an inner tumult in him, and that *and* his kiss had been intimidating. Taking one of the room keys with him had meaning, too, as though he'd said, "You might not be staying in my suite, Kate, but you're still in my territory."

Hugging herself and chafing her arms as if she were cold, Kate slowly circled the sitting room. Cooper was not a man for Katherine Redmond to be playing games with. Not that she was, but he could very easily have that impression. How did she know what he really thought about anything? How did he know with her?

Neither of them were very honest with the other. How could they ever have anything real without honesty?

It all came back in a rush of searing thoughts, the valley of her youth, the years away from Nevada, the present. How foolishly, childishly fanciful she'd been to think she could come back and make everything right! What was right, anyway? Would forcing Cooper to give up Redmond land help her grandfather?

Besides, Cooper had been completely accurate about intention. Les had intended signing away the water rights with the land, just as Sam had intended receiving them. She had it in her power to raise merry hell with Cooper about the error, but what good would it do anyone? She would never live in the valley as Cooper's enemy, not ever. And they would definitely end up bitter over a court battle.

She had made the right decision about dropping the lawsuit. As for the personal aspect of their relationship, was it even possible for her to make *any* kind of decision, right or wrong, when they were both doing their best to keep what they were really thinking and feeling locked up ridiculously tight?

Sighing, Kate went into the bedroom and eyed her suitcases. She would stay because she was close to the only man she had ever loved. And if a future with Cooper wasn't worth taking a shot at, what was?

Eleven

The phone in Kate's suite rang at 6:00 p.m. It was Cooper. "Are you all right?" he asked at once.

Kate replied as though she didn't have a care in the world, having come to one seemingly logical conclusion that afternoon: heavy, somber moods, whatever their cause or origin, were not going to help her and Cooper's relationship. "I'm *perfectly* all right. How are you doing?"

"Fine, now that I know you're okay."

He sounded harried, Kate noted, frowning slightly, wondering if her presence in the hotel wasn't adding an unnecessary dimension to Cooper's present stress. He was working doubly hard right now, which, now that she thought about it, gave his invitation another aspect for conjecture. He'd known his tight schedule when he'd invited her, and he'd wanted her here anyway.

All afternoon—during a long walk, an hour watching gamblers in the casino and a leisurely bath—Kate had played "He loves me, he loves me not," in the back of her mind. The slightest inflection in Cooper's voice, or the tiniest jab of memory, had the power to sway her one way or the other. She was on an emotional seesaw, Kate knew, alert to Cooper's every nuance.

He was speaking. "Where would you like to have dinner? Reno has some fine restaurants. We could go out, if you'd like."

"I see," Kate murmured, concealing disappointment. Eating out hadn't occurred to her. "Well, whatever you prefer is fine with me."

"What do *you* prefer?"

Detecting a thread of impatience in his voice, Kate took a breath and a plunge. "I would really prefer dinner in my suite." The phone was silent a moment, and Kate chewed her bottom lip. "Together," she hastily added when she realized Cooper could interpret her brave words to mean she wanted to eat alone.

Then she heard a quietly stated, "Great. That's what I'd prefer, too. I should be finished up very soon now. I'll order dinner for seven-thirty."

"I'll see you then."

As she had already bathed and fixed her hair and face, Kate was left with only a decision on what to wear to pass the time until dinner. Feeling no guilt about wanting to look especially feminine, Kate tried on the two cocktail dresses she had brought along to Nevada from New York. She took her time. Tonight was going to be important, she felt, maybe the most important evening of her life, and she desperately wanted to make a lasting impression. Smiling, Kate amended the thought: what she wanted to do was knock Cooper's socks off!

She had tentative plans and defined hopes for the evening ahead. They had carried on a normal conversation during lunch, and more of the same seemed highly crucial to her. There would be romance in the air, of course. Cooper and her seated at a candlelit table within the privacy of the suite was a beautifully romantic scene. Music, wine and good conversation would no doubt result in lovemaking. Which was fine with Kate. She wanted to make love with Cooper.

Only, she also wanted the preliminaries, honest give and take, some sharing of ideas, thoughts, emotions.

Settling on a black crepe dress with white satin trim, Kate pulled out gauzy black underpants and a black garter belt and laid them on the bed. To bra or not to bra? was her next debate, and with an amused smile at her small pun, she put that decision off while she donned the lingerie and sheer black hose.

Slipping into a pair of high-heeled black pumps, Kate studied herself in a full-length wall mirror. She definitely looked sexy, she absently decided, and wondered how Cooper would like seeing her this way.

"Kate."

Gasping, she turned to see Cooper standing in the doorway. His eyes were eating her up. "I knocked, but..."

"I didn't hear," she whispered breathily.

He held up the room key, then slipped it into his pants' pocket and started moving toward her. It was a hypnotizing moment, the look on his face, the sexually charged energy in the room, the memory of having just wondered how Cooper would like her dressed so seductively. Half dressed, really. *Barely* dressed. Her underpants were a mere wisp of silk chiffon, and the black garter belt, hose and pumps were outrageously suggestive.

He liked it, Kate fuzzily realized in a deluge of deliciously naughty reactions in her body. He liked it very much.

He turned her around to face the mirror again and stood behind her. His eyes were dark and smoldering and raking her reflection. Kate felt his hands rise to her waist and his body molding against hers.

She let her head fall back to his shoulder. Her pounding heart and racing pulse were physical evidence of the excitement churning within her. "I didn't expect you so soon," she whispered.

His hand moved on the side of her throat. "I got through sooner than I thought."

His clothes were different, navy slacks, a white silk shirt open at the collar. She shouldn't have dawdled with her dresses, Kate thought dizzily.

Or, from the steamy scene in the mirror, maybe she'd unknowingly done everything just right. Maybe this moment was better than anything either of them could have planned.

His hands rose to her breasts, one palm cupping each. Kate saw the heat in her own eyes and the sensual way her lips were parted. Her expression was one of blissful anticipation; Cooper's was one of rapidly increasing desire.

"You're gorgeous, fabulous," he whispered. "I probably shouldn't have walked in, but I'm glad I did."

Kate watched her lips moving, sensually shaping each word. "I'm glad you did, too." His gaze was glued to the mirror.

"This outfit is incredible."

"It's only underwear," she whispered.

"Like hell, it's only underwear," he growled. "Is this the kind of stuff you usually wear?"

"In varying colors, yes."

Cooper's hands slowly slid downward, heating her abdomen, her hips, her thighs. He was having trouble breathing normally, Kate heard.

"Garter belts rather than panty hose?" he rasped.

"I'm not comfortable in panty hose. They're too confining. I've never liked being trussed up."

He whispered in her ear. "You're terrific, beautiful, sexy. I want to make love to you in the garter belt and stockings."

Kate dampened her lips. There was a roaring in her ears. Every cell in her body was attuned to Cooper. He was making this the most erotically stimulating event of her entire life. But room service would be knocking on the door within the hour. "What about… dinner?"

The reminder seemed to daze him. It was an intrusion, an interruption. "Dinner," he finally, hoarsely repeated, and moved away. "I'll make a call. Stay right here. Don't change anything."

Kate blinked at her reflection. This wasn't going according to plan, but would she change it if she could? Cooper was on the phone, talking rapidly, issuing new orders to room service, telling someone to delay dinner until nine. In the mirror she could see him unbuttoning his shirt and shrugging it off. Apparently there was some difficulty over the menu he had previously requested. "Then we'll just have steaks. New York, medium rare. Send up all the trimmings."

Gripping the phone with his chin, he shed his pants,

shoes and socks. Kate's hand went to her throat. Cooper was down to his briefs, and so gloriously aroused, she couldn't stop staring.

The conversation was finally over. Kate could see from the expression on Cooper's face when he came up behind her again that food had completely fled his mind. He was hungry, but not for a New York steak with all the trimmings.

His hands were on her again, she leaned back against him again. Her breath was as unstable and fluttering as her heartbeat. The mirror was wildly exciting, a visual aphrodisiac, and like nothing she had ever experienced before.

Cooper's changing expressions were mesmerizing. Combined with physical sensation—his fingers tantalizing her nipples, his lips on her throat and shoulders, the pressure of his manhood on her bottom—the effect was pure dynamite on Kate.

She felt and watched him sliding her panties down, slowly, provocatively. Inch by inch, her lower body lost its chiffon covering. And then the black scrap of sheer fabric was around her ankles, a mere trifle to be kicked away.

He was whispering things, praise for her beauty, her sexuality. "You're in my blood, Katie. Do you know that? Do you know how much power you have over me?"

It was an astounding thought. Too dazed to dwell on it, Kate filed it away for later consideration. People said foolish things at such times, she knew, but mentioning power still seemed unusual to her.

Right now it didn't matter, though. Who had more power over the other was as trivial as the panties she had kicked aside. Besieged by Cooper's power, weak and trembling because of it, Kate was willing to co-operate with anything he might suggest.

And Cooper's imagination was fertile with erotic ideas. "Lean back," he whispered while his hands slid between her legs. He stared at the reflection, barely able to speak, his voice thick and guttural. "I want you here, like this."

Their eyes met in the mirror. "Protection," Kate whispered. They had taken one monumental risk, but another was too foolhardy to consider.

"You might already be pregnant."

Kate's eyes widened. Was he objecting to protection? "Wouldn't you care?"

"I'd care. The thought of you having my baby is electrifying." It was. Cooper actually felt light-headed from the thought.

Kate was bewildered. "I'll take care of protection if you insist," Cooper whispered, his lips moving against her cheek.

What was this all about? Kate was staggered by the possible implications. Did he want a child? Did he want *her*?

Oh, dear Lord, he wasn't hoping for a child just to forever heal their opposition on the valley, was he?

"Cooper, please," she mumbled, suddenly in terrible emotional pain.

His eyes bored into her in the mirror. He had upset her and damaged the sexuality of the moment. Cursing under his breath, he said, "I'll use protection. Don't move."

Kate slowly turned around as Cooper dug into his pants' pocket. Her pulse was fast and erratic. Her body was still tight and achy and demanding release. But, if anything, she understood the man she was in love with even less than she had before. Why, for God's sake, would he want to get her pregnant? *Her,* of all people?

Kate's senses reeled. Either he loved her or was seeking his own brand of justice. *His* solution to the water rights issue. In love with him or not, he was still a Sinclair, still Sam Sinclair's grandson, and old Sam would have stopped at nothing to get what he wanted. Was Cooper really so unscrupulous?

With a strange, chilling calm and very near the edge of hysteria, Kate went to the chair where she'd left her robe. She put it on, and Cooper stopped what he was doing. He had shed his shorts, about to take care of the protection Kate had wanted. "What's wrong?" he growled.

"I want to ask you something."

"Now?"

He had an incredulous look on his face, Kate saw. This scene wasn't the least bit funny, but Cooper naked and incredulous and her trembling and determined had an almost comedic feel about it just the same. Maybe it was either laugh or cry for her, Kate reasoned, but she had to forcibly halt the crazed giggle in her throat.

Cooper squinted at her, completely baffled by the almost unbelievable change in the air. With his forehead deeply marked by a perplexed frown, he pulled on his pants. "All right, ask any damned thing you want," he said gruffly.

He was angry, Kate knew. But she was beyond caring. This had gone on long enough, whatever "this" was. And if she got burned from Cooper's answers, he just might get a little scorched, too.

"I want to know what you feel for me," she said evenly, looking him right in the eye.

Cooper froze. "What do you mean?"

"What do you think I mean? That question was as simple as I could put it. Let me repeat it, just to make sure you understand." Kate spoke slowly, distinctly. "What, if anything, do you feel for me?"

His eyes narrowed. He didn't like being pinned down this way, especially on something he didn't have a clear-cut answer for. "You're trying to pick a fight, and you chose a helluva time to do it."

"I most certainly am not! *You're* trying to avoid answering, and just how should I look at that?"

Disgruntled, dismayed and frustrated, Cooper began to pace the room. "This is the damnedest thing I've ever been a part of," he muttered.

"Oh, really? Double that flattering remark for me," Kate snapped.

Stopping abruptly, Cooper gave her a hard look. "All right, I'll answer. But bear with me, because I really don't know any more about it than you do. I can't fight the chemistry between us, and I don't *want* to fight it. I want to be with you and make love with you. There's something…maybe a sense of history… between us. We share a thousand memories, and that seems important, for some reason."

Kate was standing statue-still, absorbing every word, every shading of meaning.

"There seems to be a big gap in my life, the ten years between your leaving and returning. I didn't know it while I was living it. To be brutally frank, you rarely came to mind during that period. But when I saw you again…" Cooper raked his hair. "What's this accomplishing, Kate? Do you need to hear again that

I desire you? I do. To put it crudely, you make my blood boil, my…'' He stopped. ''How blunt should I be?''

He was content with an affair. Kate's stomach turned over. She'd demanded feelings, and she'd gotten them. If Cooper was in love with her, he hadn't yet faced it.

''What about the lawsuit?'' she asked, and watched Cooper's face darken.

''I thought we had agreed not to discuss that this summer.''

''But you think about it, don't you?''

''Not very often.''

Sighing, Kate folded her arms across her chest and leaned against the dresser. She couldn't beat around the bush any longer. ''I think there's a connection between the lawsuit and our affair.''

''A connection! How could there be?''

Kate's eyes leveled on his amazed face. Something was pushing her; she couldn't stop digging. ''Why is the thought of a child by me electrifying to you? I believe that's the word you used. Why wouldn't you care if I got pregnant?''

A tension-filled moment dragged, and then a sudden understanding struck Cooper. ''You think I've been plotting some complex scenario to discourage you from suing me!'' He laughed wryly. ''God, if it were only that simple. Kate, you're crazier than a damned loon! And, by the way, thanks for the great opinion. Talk about kicking a man where it hurts. Honey, you *must* be good in court. An imagination like yours *has* to be an asset!''

Cooper picked up his shirt. ''Look, let's forget this whole thing, okay? I don't need this, Kate, especially now. For the first time, I'm getting my life in order. After this week I'll be virtually through with a business I've disliked all my life. I'm going back to the peace and quiet of the valley. I'm going to be happy, Kate, happy!''

He was buttoning his shirt. Kate was so stunned, she could only stare. Her thoughts were running wild in opposing directions. He loved her, he didn't. He was playacting, he was deeply hurt. What should she believe? What should she *do?*

"I don't suppose you want to stay for a week now," Cooper said coolly.

"Uh...no...I suppose not." She was so addled, she couldn't think straight, but staying made no sense.

"I'll have the helicopter pilot standing by in the morning. Just call the desk when you want to leave. They'll arrange transportation to the heliport."

All this because of a few questions? Kate was so wounded, she wondered if she would ever recover. Her voice was thin, reedy. "Fine...thank you."

Without another word Cooper strode from the bedroom. Kate heard the suite's door open and close, and still she couldn't move. She felt shell-shocked, she realized numbly.

All because she had dared to question him about feelings.

In his own suite Cooper dialed room service and again issued new orders. "Deliver one meal to 548 and forget the other."

He wasn't hungry; he was agitated, irritated and emotionally injured. How could Kate think he would make love to her to reduce her determination to sue him? That was the most ludicrous notion he'd ever run across!

Tearing his clothes off, Cooper climbed into bed. He was tired. A good night's sleep would do wonders. To hell with Kate's insulting opinion and innuendo!

Hours later Cooper was still wide awake and sizzlingly mad about it. He rarely had trouble sleeping. But Kate had driven him right up to the edge of an emotional precipice tonight, and he felt like he was hanging there, barely clinging to a scrap of sanity.

What was she doing now, sleeping peacefully? The possibility was more than annoying, it was infuriating.

Why had she had to delve into feelings at that particular moment? He'd been so worked up, so strung out with sexual tension. It hadn't been the right time for questions. Maybe later, after they'd made the kind of wild, uninhibited love they'd been leading up to.

Oh, yes, her bad timing had been because of that remark of his about a baby from her being an electrifying thought.

Well, it had been. Hell, it still was.

Cooper's breath stopped. *It still was!*

That's what he should have told Kate. He should have said, "Katie, maybe we should talk about something permanent. I want you to have my baby. I want…I want…"

What? What did he want? Marriage? Kate and him and children in the valley?

His eyes squeezed tightly shut. Dear God, he loved her. He loved her so much the feeling was like a physical ache deep inside of his body. He'd been afraid of her censure, of her denunciation, but why would she question him as she had unless she'd been hoping to hear that he cared and wanted more than sex from her.

"Katie," he whispered in the darkness. He had to see her, to make her understand. Right now.

Cooper got up and dressed. He ran through his suite and down the corridor. His hand was shaking when he inserted the key into the lock on Kate's door. The suite was dark and silent, although enough light was seeping in through the windows to see. He let himself in and closed the door quietly, then tiptoed through the sitting room to the open bedroom door.

He saw her small form beneath a sheet in the middle of the queen-sized bed. Her back was to him, her bare skin glistening in the dim light.

And then he heard it, a shuddering sob, and his heart stopped beating. She was sleeping, but she hadn't gone to sleep easily. How could he have said those things to her? She must have cried herself into total exhaustion.

Cooper began undressing. His clothing dropped soundlessly to the floor, piece by piece. Lifting the sheet, he carefully lowered himself onto the bed and slid up next to Kate's warm body. He curled himself around her, his nakedness melding with hers.

Instantly, even while his right hand was still sliding across Kate's waist to draw her closer, he was hard. He couldn't help the reaction. Contact with Kate was like an explosion of the senses and uncontrollable.

She stirred, and then screamed. Cooper held her down. "Don't, honey. It's only me." He felt her stiffen and try to draw away from him. "I'm sorry," he whispered. "That's why I came. I had to tell you tonight. I'm so sorry I hurt you. Katie, you mean so much to me. I know now what you were trying to do. I understand everything now, honey."

Kate was facing a window. The drapes were only

partially drawn, and a glow of neon from Reno's many signs and marquees lighted the room. Her eyes felt swollen from hours of weeping before literally passing out.

And now this, Cooper in bed with her. His gall was overwhelming, and what was he saying? That he understood everything, and that she meant so much to him? What game was he playing now?

"Leave me alone," she said dully, doubting that she could take another emotional drubbing.

"No, never. I love you, Katie." He raised to an elbow and kissed her shoulder. "I love you."

At first Kate wasn't sure she'd heard right. Maybe she was dreaming. Her mind was still foggy from too much weeping, she knew, and maybe she was imagining this whole thing.

But then Cooper's hand moved from her waist to a breast and he gyrated the hot length of his arousal against her behind. Her system went crazy. No, this wasn't a dream. It was flesh and blood and Cooper had just said he loved her!

She flopped over to her back to see his face. "What happened?"

"I did some heavy thinking."

"And you decided you love me? Just like that?"

Registering the suspicion in her voice, Cooper took her hand and kissed her fingertips. "How did you decide you love me?" He smiled. "You do, don't you?"

Dare she risk everything? Every minute, private part of herself? If she did, he would hold every ace. She would have nothing left, and he could destroy her with a word.

"How, Katie? When did you know?"

She took a shaky breath. "Ten years ago. Before that, even."

Startled, Cooper stared. "My God," he whispered. "I didn't know, Katie. Until that night by the river, I swear I..."

"It's all right. I didn't know myself, not until we took that ride to Coyote Creek." She touched his mouth, wanting to believe him very badly and yet knowing she had kept one small part of her heart in reserve. Just in case.

"Oh, Katie, what fools we've been." Cooper's head came down until their lips met, and as the kiss deepened, Kate's hands locked behind his head. A moan rose in her throat. Cooper's mouth on hers was pure heaven; his naked body against hers utter bliss.

Their mouths separated slightly. "Tell me you love me," he whispered.

"I love you, Cooper."

He grabbed her into a tight embrace, squeezing the breath out of her. "God, what took so long?" he groaned. "Why have we put each other through so much hell?"

Tears welled in her eyes, when, only a short time ago, she had thought the spring had been completely drained. "There were reasons," she huskily whispered. "We both know what they are."

"Are?" Cooper tilted his head to see her. "They're still here, those reasons?"

"Let's not talk about them now. Make love to me. I need you."

"I need you, too, more than I've ever needed anything." He put his lips in the general vicinity of her ear, nuzzling his face in her curls. "I'm on fire," he whispered. "Only you can put it out."

"Me, too. The same thing, I mean. Only you, Cooper..." Her words were stopped by a kiss of such intensity, Kate's mind ceased working. Quivering sensations took over—Cooper's wet tongue, his lips, his hands, his body. She adored every inch of the man, and proved it by touching every inch she could reach.

"There, do that again," he commanded hoarsely when her fingers found a particularly sensitive spot between his thighs. She lingered, and caressed, taking personal delight in giving him so much pleasure.

They twisted around on the bed, changing positions, kissing frantically, working themselves into a frenzy of desire. And then Cooper laid her back and positioned himself above her. Capturing her gaze, he stared into her eyes and slowly slid his aching manhood deep into the hot, moist passage of her body.

"This is only the beginning," he whispered feverishly.

"Yes, yes," she gasped.

"*Our* beginning."

The thought inched its way into that one small part of her heart she'd kept separate and inviolate. It was another doubt, but not one she could think about now. There were still areas of concern between them; confessions of love did not eradicate the realities of life.

Like using no protection again.

Closing her eyes, Kate banished worries and concentrated on the thrills spiking through her system. Making love with Cooper was a trip to the stars. Thinking about the garter belt and high heels, she smiled with feminine mystique and vowed to give him that pleasure again very soon.

He loved her. She did believe him, didn't she?

Shivering, Kate nevertheless clung and matched

Cooper's ardor. Her hips lifted to meet his seemingly tireless thrusts. They were flawless in bed, the epitome of sexual perfection. No woman could ask for a stronger, more considerate lover. And she did love him, desperately, eternally.

His skin was becoming satiny with perspiration. From his throat came masculine growls and groans, interspersed with words of love and sexuality, some of them graphic phrases that were startlingly exciting.

There was no mistaking the intensity of their relationship. They were lovers in the most primal sense. If that included real and lasting love, which it did for Kate and she prayed it did for Cooper, it was still secondary to the incredibly meaningful mating of their bodies. In this, they had no differences, no vagaries of interpretation.

They were getting close to completion, with each of them striving to give the other maximum pleasure.

But, in the end, conscious thought and effort was impossible and forgotten. Kate cried out first, nearly fainting from the force squeezing and then releasing the delicious tensions in her body. Cooper was only seconds behind, and then the glorious peace of total satisfaction descended upon them both.

Twelve

They were very near sleep, relaxed and snuggled together in Kate's bed. "You'll stay now, won't you?" Cooper murmured around a loving kiss to Kate's temple, followed immediately by a yawn he couldn't hold back.

It had come to Kate what she must do. She wasn't proud of the doubts still living in her mind, but neither could she ignore them. There was one test of Cooper's love that had to be carried out, and it could only be done in the valley because she didn't have that special document she'd drawn up along with her.

The word "test" made Kate's stomach roll. One shouldn't have to test a lover's love. But this was no ordinary boy-meets-girl-, boy-and-girl-fall-head-over-heels relationship. Far from it. There were subtleties between her and Cooper and their past that few couples could even imagine, let alone have to deal with.

Right or wrong, Kate knew she had to do it if she were ever going to have any peace of mind with Cooper.

Lifting her head, Kate planted a tender, sweetly affectionate kiss on Cooper's willing lips. "Please understand, but no, I'm not going to stay. I'll wait for you in the valley."

"Why, Katie?" he asked softly.

"Because you don't need me or any other distraction right now, mainly. But do you remember when I told you I was leaving, but had to talk to you before going?"

Cooper grimaced. "How could I forget? I still don't know what that was all about."

"I know you don't. But you will, I promise."

"You said that before, too. Kate, please don't get mysterious on me again. What we have is too important for secrets."

"Exactly. Loving you is the most important event of my life, but there's something I have to do. It's a good thing, Cooper, and nothing that will hurt you." *Oh, please let that be true!* "Will you believe that and trust me until you get home?"

Cooper emitted a long, doleful sigh. "I guess I don't have a choice, do I?"

"We always have choices," Kate said softly. "Sam had a choice ten years ago, didn't he?" She felt Cooper stiffen beside her. "Please don't get upset. We have to talk about it."

"Do we, Kate? Is it going to change the past if you and I discuss our grandfathers?"

"Nothing can alter the past, but discussion might change how we perceive it," she replied quietly.

"You mean you could end up liking Sam and I

could end up sorrier than I already was when Les lost his land?''

"You sound hard. Do you really object to talking about it so much?"

Cooper released another long breath. It was very late and he was going to be dead on his feet tomorrow. "If you stayed another day, at least, we could tear the past to shreds tomorrow night."

"You're burning the candle at both ends, as it is. Your invitation to spend the week here wasn't very practical. But if you'd really rather not talk tonight, it can wait until you return to the valley."

"Kate, you're being stubborn again."

"Maybe. But maybe you're being evasive again."

Cooper scooped her back into his arms. "Settle down, honey. I'm not being evasive—I'm beat. We'll talk when I get home. I promise on Sam's memory."

It would have to do. In seconds Cooper was sound asleep, breathing in deep, rasping breaths. He *was* beat, and she shouldn't be here when he was trying so desperately to wrap everything up.

Kate awoke to a man's hands crawling all over her. She smiled. "Impetuous in the morning?" she drawled.

"Horny is more like it." Spreading her thighs, Cooper began a gentle, circling stroke.

"Oh," she breathed, instant excitement curling within her. "Should I expect this sort of thing every morning we wake up together?"

"You should." Cooper bent his head to kiss her, and she realized that he had already showered and brushed his teeth.

"Wait a darned minute here," Kate cried. "You've already been up."

"Is it my fault you're a sleepyhead?"

Kate bounced up and off the bed. "Give me three minutes. Time them!" Dashing into the bathroom, she turned on the shower and took her toothbrush into the stall with her. No way was she going to kiss Cooper with a less than sweet-smelling breath. No way!

"You took four minutes," Cooper teased when she returned to the bed. He held up the sheet and welcomed her damp body. This time, when he attempted to kiss her, Kate's lips were parted and inviting.

They kissed and touched each other for lovely long minutes, losing the sheet somewhere along the way. And then they were making love again, with Cooper on top and sliding in and out of her at a dizzying pace.

"You *are* impetuous in the morning," Kate whispered thickly.

"Do you like it?"

She pulled his head down and kissed him, pushing her tongue into his mouth. She was obsessed with this man, Kate knew, and if things didn't work out, she was in for one hell of a lonely, heartbroken future.

The kiss went on and on, an intoxicating accompaniment to the rhythmic thrusts of their bodies. "If I didn't like it, I wouldn't be lying underneath you, my love," she whispered raggedly when they came up for air.

His eyes were dark and daring. "How about on top of me?"

Kate's pulse leaped. "For a change of pace?"

"I've got quite a few ideas on the subject, sweetheart. Stay for the week, and we'll try them all out."

She let the invite pass. She wasn't going to stay,

but there were more urgent things going on now than another debate on that matter. If everything *did* work out, they would have years to try every one of Cooper's wonderfully naughty ideas.

"Let me get on top," she whispered, purposely seductive.

A hot light ignited his eyes, and he rolled away from her and laid on his back. His sex was wet and visibly throbbing. "You're a sexy guy," Kate commented throatily, and positioned herself over him, one leg on either side of his hips.

"And you're a sexy lady. Sit down slowly, honey."

It was an incredible sensation. He was fully and deeply inside of her. She leaned forward, bringing her breasts down to his lips. His mouth opened around one, and the gentle sucking action she felt shot throughout her body in a feverish wave of desire.

She lifted her hips, then dropped back again. It felt deliriously exciting. "Do you have time for this?" she whispered.

"No. But do it as long as you want to, baby. Do it for three days if that's what you want."

"Three days?" Kate laughed huskily. "A rather ambitious project, don't you think?"

Cooper's eyes sobered. "Make it last, honey."

She nodded slowly, knowing full well it couldn't last very long. Not with him suckling her nipples and fingering the very core of her feminity.

If one were crass enough to think of that power stuff at a time like this, the top of one's head just might explode, Kate thought dreamily. Being the aggressor, the master of the game, was pretty heady. She suspected Cooper had many more such tricks up his sexual sleeve, and she wanted to be a part of each and every one of them.

She would be, too—if he really did love her.

He began clutching her hips, directing her slides. "A little faster," he mumbled, his eyes becoming glazed with passion. "This is fantastic."

"Yes," she panted, raising and lowering faster. And then the first spasm came in a meltdown that drained her to weakness. "Cooper," she gasped, falling against him.

Quickly he tipped her over. His thrusts were hard and fast, and his cry of release echoed throughout the room.

He rested a few deliciously lazy minutes, then lifted his head. "I love you more than I ever thought it was possible to love anyone, Katie. It took so long for me to get serious about a woman. Was I waiting for you to come back?"

"Oh, Cooper," she whispered, too shaken to even speak normally. Each time they made love was better than the last.

Cooper's eyes were dark blue and pleading. "Stay, Kate. All day, whatever else I'll be doing, I'll know you'll be here tonight."

Her hands rose to his face. "It's best if I don't. A few days apart will give us both a chance to think, anyway."

"Think about what? I've done enough thinking. I want you in my bed tonight."

"I'll be in the valley, Cooper. Think of me there, waiting for you. That's exciting, too. I'll be thinking of you coming home."

"You're not going to change your mind about staying, are you?"

"No, Cooper," she said gently. "I have to do this.
You don't need any diversions this week, not even me
in your bed at night. And I promise you'll understand
everything when you get home."

The week was finally over. Cooper had packed his
personal belongings—books, mementos, clothing—in
boxes to be shipped to the ranch, and he walked
through the suite he had occupied for years for one
final look around. The gym equipment wouldn't be
needed any longer. Physical labor, which he fully intended doing from now on, would take the place of
pulleys and springs. Cooper grinned and closed the
door on the room.

Everything was fine. The staff had given him a retirement party last night, and a few tears had been
shed. He'd heard some nice things about himself, the
usual goodbye speeches, he'd figured at first. But then
it had gotten to him, the handshakes, the kisses, the
slaps on the back. His people genuinely regretted his
break with the business.

It was the only aspect of deserting Sinclair's that
meant a damn. He'd be back periodically until the
place was sold, he'd told everyone in his own goodbye
speech. And in a burst of emotional generosity, he'd
promised everyone a bonus with their next paycheck.

It was the only thing he'd been able to come up
with to appease his conscience with employees who
had been honest and fair with him. Standing on that
dais, with hundreds of faces looking up at him, Cooper
had received a standing ovation with that announcement. The evening had turned out well.

Going to the door, Cooper glanced back at the elegant suite. Jack Leonard and his wife would be using

it now, and no doubt Norma would make some changes.

That was fine, too. *Everything* was fine. He was going home! Cooper closed the door.

Whistling a tuneless melody, he headed for the elevator, patting his breast jacket pocket as he went. He wasn't looking for a cigarette, either. No sirree! What was in that pocket was a hundred times, a *thousand* times more important than a damned cigarette.

It was an insurance policy, Cooper thought with a jubilant laugh, giving the Down button a tap. A piece of paper with the power to convince Kate once and for all how much he loved her could be labeled an insurance policy, couldn't it?

Still chuckling, Cooper entered the elevator. Jack was meeting him downstairs for a final handshake, and then he was flying to Mustang Valley.

And to Kate.

Or maybe he was flying to Kate first and the valley second.

Then again, maybe they were one and the same in meaning.

Kate was as nervous as a spooked cat, prowling the house, puttering, glancing out the windows every few minutes. The water rights document resided on the coffee table in plain sight. She was going to give it to Cooper the minute he arrived.

That's when she would know exactly how he felt about her. When he read that document and learned there was no longer any chance of a lawsuit, she would know his true priorities by his expression.

And she was scared stiff about it. He'd said repeatedly that he loved her and had kissed her senseless before she left Reno. But that small icy spot in her heart just wouldn't melt, no matter how often or how ardently she tried to heat it up with memories and mental debates in Cooper's favor.

The mistrust she couldn't expunge from her system boiled down to Cooper's name, Kate knew, to genetics. Old Sam Sinclair had been an unscrupulous scoundrel, and Cooper had the same blood flowing through his veins. That's what Kate couldn't stop worrying about.

She had another worry, too. Her period was three days late. No wonder she was walking the floor and wringing her hands, she thought again, having reached that conclusion too many times to count already that day.

There were so many ifs to ponder, so many directions her life could go after today. *If* she was pregnant and Cooper didn't really love her, what would she do? Tell him he was going to be a father by long distance from New York?

It was much too soon to be thinking those things, Kate knew. Her periods weren't always regular, and three days was nothing to get alarmed about.

Finding herself in the kitchen, Kate yanked open the refrigerator door to get a cold drink. And then she heard it, the distant but unique sound of a helicopter. Her pulse went crazy and she suddenly felt on the verge of hyperventilation.

Her hands clenched into fists, which she placed on her forehead. "Calm down," she commanded herself fiercely. "Just calm down! He'll walk in here and see a basket case. Will that help anything?"

Filling a glass with water, Kate washed down two aspirin tablets, then refilled the glass and took it out to the porch. She sat down and sipped the water. She wanted to greet Cooper with at least a semblance of dignity, a precaution, really. A matter of self-protection. She was terribly vulnerable right now, and if things didn't work out...?

Weary of that shattering speculation, Kate turned her thoughts to a more mundane subject. Did she look all right? Her dress was sunflower yellow and pretty. She had taken great pains with her hair and makeup. At least twenty times already, she had checked her appearance in a mirror.

Finally Kate set the glass down and closed her eyes, directing her thoughts to an imaginary place where discord, worries and anxiety didn't exist. It was an exercise she sometimes practiced before an extraordinarily trying court case. Meditation was as old as civilization, but Kate hadn't tried it until a colleague suggested it to her one time when she was particularly edgy about a difficult presentation.

It wasn't a guarantee of serenity for Kate as she definitely hadn't mastered the art. But today it seemed to be relaxing a little of her tension, a blessing.

She was still on the porch when a car drove into the driveway. In a heartbeat, dignity and worry and everything else was forgotten. Kate was up on her feet, leaping off the porch, dashing around the house. Cooper got out of the car and held his arms open.

They collided about halfway between the house and his car. "Oh, Katie, Katie." Kisses fell everywhere, on lips, on cheeks, on throats. They were laughing and exchanging endearments, and kissing and kissing.

Breathless, Kate tilted her head back. "You're finally home. How does it feel?"

Hugging her to his side, Cooper started them walking toward the back of the house. "Like a miracle, Katie. It feels just like a miracle."

Her arm was around his waist, her other hand on his chest. "And you don't have to rush right back to Reno. Oh, Cooper, I'm so happy for you."

She was; he could see it in her eyes. "We've got some plans to make, Katie."

Plans? Kate's heart fluttered in her chest. Maybe she already knew Cooper's love wasn't an act. Maybe the test wasn't at all necessary. Was she going too far?

They rounded the back corner of the house and then climbed the stairs to the porch. Cooper's handsome face was expectant, exhilarated. He was happy to be home and thrilled to see her. Kate's previous determination was wilting fast. Why was she so bogged down in the past? Why couldn't she just accept the present and forget Sam and yes, even Les?

She couldn't go through with it, she realized with a low sensation in the pit of her stomach. She would give Cooper the document as a gift, not as a damned test. And she would accept whatever happened afterward, too.

Her voice had lost most of its lilt when she said unsteadily, "Before we talk about anything else, I've got something to give you."

Cooper exhibited a pleased-as-punch smile. "I've got something to give you, too. Hey, what is this, Christmas or something?"

Looking at him, Kate's heart felt close to bursting with love. She moved nearer and slid her hands up his chest to the back of his neck. "I love you, Cooper," she whispered. That sliver of ice in her chest had vanished, she knew. She was through with games, tests, doubts and self-induced misery, giving everything she was now, every tiny, private part of herself. She had nothing left that belonged to her alone.

His arms closed around her. His warmth, his very essence seeped through Kate's skin and deeply embedded itself into her system. For a long, wonderfully moving time they stood there, just holding one another.

This was no act, Kate realized with tears burning her eyes. No one could pretend the kinds of feelings she was picking up from Cooper. She'd been so wrong, so horribly, inexcusably wrong.

"Come," she whispered. "Let me give you my gift. It will explain everything."

Cooper smiled down at her, then saw her swimming eyes. His smile disappeared as quickly as it had come. "It's not a goodbye gift, is it?"

Kate stared. Why, he was as uncertain about her as she was about him! Selfishly she had never once thought of Cooper's side of this, not from a truly sincere standpoint. Of course, that was the problem: she hadn't believed his sincerity. In all honesty, she hadn't believed a Sinclair *could* be sincere.

"Oh, Cooper," she sighed sadly. "I've made so many mistakes."

_ "Don't tell me you're leaving, Kate, please." His tone was anxious, his eyes uneasy.

She wiped the moisture away from her cheeks and shaped a smile. "Only one thing could make me leave, if you asked me to."

Shoulders slumping in obvious relief, Cooper vigorously exclaimed, "Ask you to! Well, that's one thing that will never happen. Look at this, Kate." Reaching into his inside coat pocket, he came out with an envelope, which he placed in Kate's hand. "This is for you, Katie. Because I love you, and because I want you to…" He grinned. "I'm not saying any more until you see what it is."

Kate curiously scanned the plain white envelope. She couldn't begin to guess at its contents, which, from its thinness, wasn't any more than one sheet of paper.

"Open it," Cooper urged.

"Yes, all right." Kate lifted the envelope's flap and extracted a folded paper. With her trained eye, it took less than two seconds to grasp the document's meaning. "My Lord," she whispered, lifting her gaze to Cooper's. "You've signed over Granddad's land to me."

Cooper was grinning from ear to ear. "It's yours. I had Dave Walker draw up that deed right after you left." Cooper hadn't been positive about what to expect from Kate at this moment, but why was she laughing?

It had started with a smile, then a small laugh, and now she was laughing so hard, she had to hold on to the porch railing to stay on her feet. She wiped her eyes, looked at the deed and began whooping again. Puzzled, Cooper emitted a bit of laughter himself, but he was too genuinely perplexed at Kate's reaction to really join in.

Then, without warning, she threw herself into his arms. "Oh, Cooper, Cooper. If you only knew," she managed before burying her face in his shirt and choking with laughter again.

He stroked her hair and back. Apparently, he thought happily, she was overjoyed with his gift. It was several more minutes before she had calmed down to only an occasional spurt of giggles. But, even wrig-

gling with laughter, she felt wonderful in his arms, and
he held her with pleasure and a lovely contentment
coursing through his veins.

Finally she stepped back. "Come into the living
room and see *my* gift," she invited, the tremor of her
lips threatening another bout of hilarity.

Cooper nodded. "Is it going to make *me* laugh?"
he teased.

"I wouldn't doubt it," she said with another giggle.

It occurred to Cooper on the short walk through the
house that he couldn't remember Kate ever being a
giggler. Something was tickling her funny bone, something he couldn't even begin to surmise.

Her eyes were impish with deviltry when she lifted
a piece of paper off the coffee table and handed it to
him. Mystified, Cooper accepted it and began reading.
It took him a little longer than it had Kate to digest
the legalese. When he had, he looked at Kate with a
dismayed expression.

She smiled. "Do you remember the O. Henry story
about the Christmas gifts exchanged by a poor, young
married couple? I believe it was titled *The Gift of the
Magi*. The young wife sold her beautiful long hair to
buy her husband a watch fob, and he sold his watch
to buy her a special comb for her hair."

"Katie, you've given me your water rights," Cooper said in a stunned, benumbed voice.

"And you gave me your land."

"But...why?"

"Look at the date on the document, Cooper. I had
decided against the lawsuit and was planning to go
back to New York. That's what was behind that request I made to see you before I left. I was going to

give you that document and ask if you would buy my hundred acres.''

"A complete break with the valley," Cooper murmured. His eyes narrowed on her. "What changed your mind, making love the way we did?"

"I…was having difficulty with it even before that," she admitted. Her eyes sought his. "I knew I was in love with you, and I thought…"

"That I was using you to discourage the lawsuit."

He wasn't angry about it, nor astonished, as he'd been in Reno. Grateful, Kate spoke with confidence, "Yes."

Cooper looked down at the paper in his hand. He shook his head. "This is the damnedest thing I've ever heard of." He grinned, then laughed.

"It *is* funny, isn't it?" Kate asked, praying that he really did see the irony of the exchanged gifts as something to laugh about.

Eliminating the space between them in two strides, Cooper wrapped his arms around her. "It's funny, yes, but it's also pretty damned significant. I guess love brings out the best in people. I want you to have that land, Kate. I want you to feel at home here."

Kate stole a breath. "I have the money for Granddad's old debt."

His eyes darkened. "Don't even think it. The last thing I need is more money."

His face was so dear to her, Kate couldn't resist touching it. She would repay the old loan, of course, but she couldn't argue about that now. Her hand rose and tenderly caressed his cheek. "You're not at all like Sam. How could I have been so mistaken?"

It startled her when Cooper took both of her hands in his and held them. "I'm very much like Sam, Katie,'' he said with quiet but unmistakable firmness. ''I'm also very *proud* of being like him.''

Her heart began a heavy thudding. ''No, I see differences,'' she rebutted huskily, suddenly frightened at this strange turn.

''Some, yes. I don't like gambling and Sam did, which is probably the most obvious difference. But underneath, Katie, inside, I'm a lot like Sam.''

She didn't want to hear this. Backing up, her eyes wide and bewildered, she denied it again. ''You're not, don't say that!''

''Does that idea make you love me less? Kate, I want you to marry me. I'm *asking* you to marry me.''

Breathing hard, as though she'd done something physically straining, Kate took another backward step.

''We love each other, Katie. Maybe we always did. If you'd been older ten years ago, or if you hadn't left the valley, we might have figured that out a long time ago.''

''I didn't leave voluntarily!''

''No, I know you didn't. You did what you had to do. So did Sam, and Les, and even me. Don't keep judging the past, honey. Love me, marry me, have my babies. Let's fill Mustang Valley with boisterous, beautiful kids. Let's be happy, Katie.''

Could she forget? Could she bear and raise Sam Sinclair's great-grandchildren without remembering that old villain's unscrupulous tactics every time she looked at her own babies?

But they would be Les's great-grandchildren, too. And Cooper's children. Her beloved Cooper.

My God, she was trying to carry that old feud into another generation! Was she totally demented? Cooper had proposed, for heaven's sake, *proposed!*

Kate flew across the room and literally jumped on Cooper. Laughing, he caught her with perfect timing. Her legs went around his hips and her arms around his neck, and she began kissing every millimeter of his face. "Yes, yes, yes," she breathlessly got in between mad, impassioned kisses.

Backing up to the sofa, Cooper brought them both down on a saggy old cushion. He wasn't laughing anymore. "I love you, Katie." His mouth settled on hers in a beautifully drugging kiss.

She was straddling his lap, facing him. Their lips inched apart, their gazes meeting. "I'm sorry," Kate whispered. "Sorry for doubting you, sorry for comparing you to anyone, even your own grandfather. You're uniquely you, Cooper, and I love you just the way you are."

"I know you'll never really forgive Sam, Katie. But someday, not for a while, but later, when we're settled and completely comfortable with one another, then I want you to get to know Sam better."

Kate studied the man she loved so much. "How?"

"I've got an entire room of memorabilia at the ranch, letters he wrote and received, photographs, news articles, and some old journals he kept. Kate, not everyone got to know Sam the way I did. I'm not trying to convince you he was a saint. But who is?" Cooper's voice lowered. "Was Les?"

"A saint? Granddad?" Kate nearly laughed. The thought of Les Redmond as a saint was really a riot. He'd been the swearingest, drinkingest, hell-on-wheels man she'd ever known. In later years he'd calmed down, but Kate well remembered how cocky and full of the devil he'd been in his younger days. "No," she said, smiling at a torrent of memories. "He wasn't a saint, either."

Sighing, Cooper laid his head back against the sofa. "I'm so glad to be home, Kate. If it were possible, I'd never leave Mustang Valley again for anything." His eyes moved across the drab, faded wallpaper and scarred woodwork of the room. Kate had scrubbed and painted what she could, but it would take more than soap and paint to restore this old house. That was another subject to talk about later on. Kate could do what she wanted with the place; it meant nothing beyond her feelings for it to Cooper.

A daring, exciting idea was forming in Kate's mind. Leaning forward, she kissed his sexy mouth and whispered, "Give me five minutes alone in the bedroom and then come in, okay?"

"Another gift?"

She batted her eyelashes at him. "One could say that, I suppose. See you in five minutes, handsome."

He held on to her. "First, before you go, when can we be married?"

A slow smile broke out on Kate's face. "Tomorrow?"

Laughing joyously, Cooper pulled her into a bear hug. "Tomorrow it is. Now, run along and get into that black garter belt and high heels."

Kate's mouth dropped open. "How did you…?"

He only smiled.

Epilogue

"Got a minute, Kate?"

She looked up from the tiny garments she was folding. "Sure, Dirk." The laundry room was big enough for more than one person. "Come on in."

"Thanks."

Kate gave the lanky cowboy a smile. "What can I do for you?"

"Coop said...well, I mentioned it to him, and he said to talk to you about it."

"Oh?" Kate added another tiny undershirt to a growing stack.

Dirk shuffled his feet, obviously uncertain. "Uh... it's about that fenced-in hundred acres. I...I'd like to buy it."

The young man had blurted that out as if he feared Kate leaping at him and smacking him with a diaper! She laughed. "Don't be so uncomfortable, Dirk. After two years I think we're good enough friends to talk about most things, don't you?''

''Well, sure, but when I mentioned it to Coop...''

''He was positive I would say no?''

''He didn't say much of anything about it, Kate,'' Dirk replied hastily, as if to assure Kate that her husband wasn't even capable of attempting to make a decision for her. It brought another smile to Kate's lips.

She went on folding and stacking. Two babies went through an enormous amount of clothing every day, she'd learned. *Two* babies, twin boys. Robert Lester and Thomas Samuel were such a miracle, Kate walked on air most of the time.

''What would you do with it, Dirk? A hundred acres would only support a handful of cattle.''

Dirk's face became eager. ''It's the house I want, Kate.'' His expression quickly changed to chagrin. ''I rushed in here too fast, I think. But when Coop said he'd consider selling me nine hundred acres...''

''Ah, I see,'' Kate murmured. ''And you and Cooper just had that little talk?''

''This morning.'' Embarrassed, his face red, Dirk started easing to the door. ''I don't know what I was thinking,'' he mumbled. ''Sorry, Kate.''

''We haven't had a chance to talk about anything yet today, Dirk,'' Kate said gently. ''We'll discuss it this evening, I promise.''

''Thanks, Kate.''

When Dirk had gone, Kate continued folding laundry. Sell the old house? Hmm, she thought, frowning slightly. She'd done nothing with it, but still...

These days Kate had little time for trips into the past. She took care of her babies herself, having refused Cooper's generous offer of a nurse. "Our babies are going to know their parents," she'd told him, and every day something happened that proved how happy Cooper was with her decision.

They were both happy, Kate acknowledged serenely while she carried an armful of tiny things to the nursery. Leila was still the head housekeeper, an important part of the Sinclair family. Just as Dirk was. Cowhands came and went, but Dirk loved the valley as much as she and Cooper did.

Sell the house. Wouldn't it be better for someone to be using it than for it to be sitting there empty and deteriorating?

Of course it would be, but what about those undefined plans she'd had for restoring it?

The seed Dirk had planted sprouted all afternoon. One minute Kate would see the sense of someone living in the house, and the next, sentimentality would grip her.

She was still undecided when Cooper came in for dinner. As was usual at the end of his work day, he was dirty, sweaty and grinning. There wasn't a happier man alive, Kate was positive. Sinclair's, in Reno, had been sold and was now only a memory. She had taken the Nevada bar examination and passed, but any plans for going back to work were nebulous and way, way down on her list of priorities. Someday, maybe, was the way Kate thought of it. Already, with the twins only four months old, she was thinking about another baby.

So was Cooper. "A girl, honey. We really need a little girl."

"Maybe two?" Kate had asked dryly.

"Now that would really be something, wouldn't it? Two sets of twins?"

"Do you know what the odds are of having a second set of twins?"

They had both burst out laughing at that. Any reference to gambling always seemed funny to them. Gifts were another subject that never failed to raise laughter. They laughed a lot these days, laughed and talked and loved one another and the babies.

Kate was in the nursery when Cooper stuck his head in. "Shh," she whispered with a finger to her lips. He tiptoed in and looked down at first one sleeping infant, then the other, his eyes glowing with adoration.

Hand in hand, they silently left the room. Kate positioned the door just so, about six inches ajar, and they walked across the hall to their private suite.

As smooth as silk, they glided into one another's arms. Cooper sighed with complete contentment and kissed the top of his wife's head.

Standing so, Kate felt the heat gathering in her belly. Her breasts were much larger than before the babies, her waist a little thicker, her hips fuller. She had become a completely wanton creature, she knew, so sexually attuned to her husband, just touching him brought desire.

"Hmm," she murmured, nuzzling her face in his throat, her arms wrapped tightly around his waist.

"I'm dirty," he whispered, his husky voice reflecting his own developing desire.

Kate's lips nibbled at his. "I need you."

His hands slid to her bottom, drawing their lower bodies closer. "Take a shower with me."

"You're just full of great ideas." Laughing softly, Kate took his hand and led him to the bathroom. They shed their clothes quickly, watching the other, their excitement mounting. Cooper reached into the large tiled stall and turned the water on. He held out a hand.

While Cooper shampooed his hair, Kate soaped his back. Then he turned around. She lathered his chest, smiling at the designs she was making in its triangle of hair. Neither was smiling a few minutes later. The shower stall was steamy from hot water and pure unadulterated lust.

"Oh, how I love you," she gasped when he entered her.

"Oh, Katie, Katie. It only gets better and better," he groaned hoarsely. Reaching behind himself, he turned off the water, then lifted Kate off the floor, bringing her legs around his hips. His thrusts began strong and sure, and he watched the play of emotion on his wife's beautiful face.

His wife, his Katie, the mother of his babies. Cooper felt tears in his eyes. Sometimes he was so overcome with emotion with Kate, he couldn't help tears. He placed his head alongside hers, their wet hair tangling, and loved her with his heart, soul and body.

Her cry of fulfillment was music to his ears and only seconds before his. Sated and trembling, he lowered her feet to the shower floor and held her. "I love you seems inadequate," he said raggedly. "How did I get so lucky?"

"We, darling, we."

Their kiss was tender, filled with love. Then, smiling at one another, they got out of the shower and began toweling off. Kate grimaced at her reflection. "My hair's a mess."

Grinning, Cooper ruffled her wet curls. "A gorgeous mess." His gaze slid down her ripe body. "You're gorgeous all over."

"I'm getting fat."

Cooper's hand closed around a breast. "Not fat, voluptuous."

Kate laughed. "A few more babies and you might not be so kind."

Cooper drew her into his arms, his expression sober. "Nothing could make me love you less than I do, least of all a few pounds. You'll still be beautiful to me when we're hobbling around with canes."

She smiled softly and touched his face. "I do love you so very, very much." They stood there, basking in their emotions for another minute, then began dressing.

In the bedroom, Kate remembered Dirk's request. "Apparently you and Dirk discussed selling him some of the valley this morning."

Cooper nodded while buttoning his shirt. "He asked, honey. I told him you and I would have to talk about it before I could give him an answer. Did he mention your house, too?"

"Yes, he did. I've been having trouble with that this afternoon."

"You don't have to sell it, you know."

"I know, but it seems so silly to hang onto it. Even if I renovated it, what would I do with it?"

Cooper shoved the tail of his shirt into his clean jeans. "I think our first decision is whether or not to sell any part of the valley. How do you feel about that?"

Kate frowned. "It's always been owned by our families. I just don't know. How do *you* feel about it?"

At a mirror, Cooper brushed his hair. "He wants to get married, Kate."

"To Beth?"

Cooper grinned. "Of course, to Beth. They've been practically inseparable for a year now."

"Why didn't he tell me that?"

Shrugging, Cooper sat down on the bed to dress his feet. "You know Dirk. He's not much of a talker."

Kate was dressed and pacing. "I really like Beth, don't you?"

"I like them both. Dirk's a good man."

Kate went to the window. From this spot she could see the top story of her old house at the other end of the valley. It suddenly looked deserted and forlorn to her eyes. "We have so much, you and I," she murmured. Beth Ferguson was a nice young woman and obviously madly in love with Dirk.

Turning abruptly, her eyes sparkling, Kate exclaimed, "Let's do it, Cooper. Let's give them their chance. We won't even miss that thousand acres."

Cooper grinned. "I thought you'd come to that conclusion." Rising, he walked over to Kate and put his arms around her. After a kiss, he looked down at her. "I think it would be best if you drew up the deed, counselor." A teasing twinkle shone in his eyes. "We wouldn't want to overlook conveying the water rights along with the land, would we?"

"No, we certainly wouldn't want to do that," Kate replied solemnly.

They stared at each other, then broke up with laughter.

* * * * *

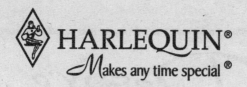

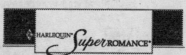

Where love comes alive™

From first love to forever, these love stories are
for today's woman with traditional values.

A highly passionate, emotionally powerful
and always provocative read.

SPECIAL EDITION™

Emotional, compelling stories that capture the
intensity of living, loving and creating a family in
today's world.

INTIMATE MOMENTS™

A roller-coaster read that delivers romantic thrills
in a world of suspense, adventure and more.

Visit Silhouette at www.eHarlequin.com

SDIR2